GEORGES SIMENON

The Krull House

Translated by HOWARD CURTIS

PENGUIN BOOKS

PENGUIN CLASSICS

UK | USA | Canada | Ireland | Australia
India | New Zealand | South Africa

Penguin Books is part of the Penguin Random House group of companies
whose addresses can be found at global.penguinrandomhouse.com.

First published in French as *Chez Krull* by Gallimard 1939
This translation first published 2018
001

Set in 11.25/14 pt Dante MT Std
Typeset by Jouve (UK), Milton Keynes
Printed in Great Britain by Clays Ltd, St Ives plc

ISBN: 978-0-241-32069-3

The Krull House

1.

The first thing that Hans – a Krull himself, but a pure one, a German Krull – saw of the Krull house, the Krull family, even before he got out of the taxi, was a transparent paper sign stuck to the glass door of the shop.

It was odd: with all the details calling for his attention, he had eyes only for that sign, two words he managed to read backwards. 'Remy Starch.'

The background was blue, a beautiful ultramarine blue, and the middle of the image was occupied by a peaceable white lion.

At that moment, the rest existed only in relation to that lion, its mane as spotless as linen: another sign, also transparent, with the words 'Reckitt's Laundry Blue', although this one, for no clear reason, played only a minor role; another word, 'Drinks', painted in yellow, some of the letters on the left-hand pane of the door, the others on the right; a window cluttered with ropes, lanterns, horsewhips and harnesses; finally, somewhere in the sun, there was a canal, trees, motionless barges and a yellow tram advancing along the quayside, ringing its bell.

'*Remy Starch!*' Hans spelled as he got out of the taxi.

The words seemed all the more emblematic in that Hans didn't understand French very well and had no idea what they meant.

'Let's see what these French Krulls are like!' he thought as he stuffed the change in his pocket and looked up at the house.

Above the shop, a window was open, and through it he glimpsed the top half of a young man in shirtsleeves sitting at a table covered in exercise books. From another part of the house, heavy piano chords emerged.

And now, beyond the window display of nautical items, in a half-light that seemed a long way away, Hans made out a woman's forehead, grey hair, eyes. At the same moment, the young man in shirtsleeves was framed in the first-floor window, looking down curiously at the taxi; another window, to the right, opened to reveal a young girl's sharp face . . .

There were only three metres of pavement to cross, and a glass door to open. In his left hand, Hans carried a yellow leather suitcase – imitation leather, to be precise, but it was a decent imitation, the kind the Germans were good at producing. Being tall, he took long strides. One. Two. He was reaching out his hand to turn the door handle when the door swung open and an extraordinary voice, a woman's voice, but hoarse and with a cacophonous mixture of highs and lows, screamed out over all the other sounds:

'You're a pervert and you know it! You're all perverts in this house! Not just thieves, dirty little thieves, but perverts!'

Hans, his suitcase in his hand, had to mark time while the two women jostled in the doorway, one shaking the other and trying to push her out, the second determined to finish her monologue.

One word had struck Hans, the word 'pervert' – he thought he knew the meaning, but he didn't see how it could apply to a family with the name Krull. Then another word, uttered by the grey-haired shopkeeper, who was probably his aunt:

'Come on, Pipi, let's not have a scene!'

And that word – Pipi – lodged itself in his memory alongside Remy Starch.

All this had lasted the time it took him to get out of the taxi, pay the driver and cross the pavement. The young man from the first floor was already emerging from the shop, grabbing the drunk woman by one arm and shoving her violently enough to make her stagger several metres.

'Hans Krull?' he asked, taking the traveller's suitcase.

'That's me, yes,' Hans replied in German.

In spite of everything, it took a while to get used to the situation: his aunt was looking him up and down, but it was clear that what most struck her was the suitcase with its dazzling nickel-plating.

'Come in,' the young man said, throwing a last threatening look at the woman they had called Pipi.

Then there was the smell. Not immediately, though: before anything else, there was the bell. Whenever the door opened and closed, a bell would ring, a sound that made you feel you had never heard anything like it before.

Only then, once you were in the shop, came the smell, a mixture of Norwegian tar – used to coat the barges – rope and spices, but predominantly the hard liquor sold on a corner of the counter that had been covered in zinc.

'Come into the lounge, cousin. We didn't think you'd take a taxi. Anna! Élisabeth! Cousin Hans is here!'

Behind the shop, Hans glimpsed a kitchen, which he sensed was the real centre of the house, but he was made to turn right and walk down a chilly corridor paved with large blue tiles and into the lounge, where a young girl hurriedly got up from the piano stool.

'Hello, cousin.'

'Hello.'

'This is Élisabeth, my father calls her Liesbeth . . . This is Anna . . . And I'm Joseph.'

'Don't you speak any French?' Élisabeth asked while her mother, her hands over her belly, remained motionless in the doorway.

'Not much, and very badly. You'll teach me.'

All initiations are unpleasant, yet Hans kept his good humour, a characteristic good humour that they were unfamiliar with in the house. It was a lightness of both body and mind. He moved with ease, as graceful as a dancer, while his eyes, which were small, twinkled with delight and, perhaps, mischief.

'Would you like me to show you your room, cousin?' Joseph said. He was about the same age as Hans – twenty-five – but his movements were stiff and heavy.

The stairs, which were polished, creaked. The whole house exuded the same smell as the shop, though less strong; it mingled with more domestic odours upstairs. The window on the landing looked out on a yard and a garden with a single tree.

'This way, cousin. It's an attic room, but it has a view of the canal . . . Wouldn't you like to have a quick wash?'

Hans looked at his hands, which were perfectly clean. He smiled and almost explained why. Should he say it?

Not yet! he decided. Later, he might tell him that, on the train from Cologne, he had made the acquaintance of a pretty woman and had helped her to smuggle some objects across the border. On getting off at the station, he had taken her to the railway hotel.

It was the kind of adventure that constantly happened to him, almost without his doing it deliberately. She hadn't even undressed. She had said:

'My sister-in-law is expecting me at half past four, and my husband will be back at six . . .'

That was why he had washed before coming to the Krulls'. He hadn't even asked her what her name was. She had got on a yellow tram.

'You've seen almost the whole family,' Joseph explained conscientiously as his cousin opened his suitcase and took out a few small objects. 'Mother takes care of the shop . . .'

'Why did she call that woman Pipi? Is that her name?'

'No, it's a nickname! That woman's the bane of my mother's life. She lives with her daughter and a tramp on an abandoned barge that's half sunk into the canal. She runs errands for the bargees, especially those that are passing through and only spend a few minutes in the lock. She's drunk all day long and when she feels the urge, she just crouches down by the edge of the water or in the street and relieves herself.'

'I get the idea.'

'My sister Anna, who's the oldest—'

'How old?'

'Thirty! She's the one who looks after the house. When you arrived, she was ironing in the kitchen . . . Élisabeth is seventeen. She's studying piano. She wants to be a teacher.'

'And you?'

'I'm studying to be a doctor. In two weeks' time, I'll be presenting my thesis on bilateral pneumothorax.'

'What about your father?'

'He spends all day in the workshop with his assistant . . . Shall we go and see him?'

The workshop was a room at the end of the ground-floor corridor, with a door that led out to the garden. Two men, sitting on chairs so low they might have been sitting on the floor, were weaving wicker into baskets.

One of them – with his fine white beard, he looked like a statue of Saint Joseph – was Old Krull, Cornelius Krull, the one who, after travelling first around Germany, then around France as a basket-maker, had settled in this town, for no reason, like a man automatically stopping when he's reached the end of his journey.

Instead of kissing Hans on the forehead, he traced a little cross there with his thumb, in a gesture that was typical of him, then asked:

'How's my brother?'

'He's well,' Hans replied brightly, 'quite well.'

'Does he still live in our house in Emden? In the last letter I had from him, thirty years ago, he told me he'd set up as a cobbler.'

Cornelius Krull, with his impassive face and solid beard, continued to manipulate the flexible wicker stems, while a quid of chewing tobacco swelled now the left cheek, now the right cheek of his assistant, his only employee, who was as much of a fixture in the house as Old Krull himself.

'Would you like to see my room now, cousin?'

It smelled musty. It was the most disagreeable of the smells in the house, and Joseph was boring, with his long, insubstantial body, his pale, constantly serious face, his close-cropped hair, between fair and ginger, and his dull blue eyes.

'Are you studying, too?'

'I was studying law. I was forced to leave university for political reasons.'

'What do you do in Germany?'

'Nothing. I'm never going back to Germany.'

He sensed Joseph's gaze turning cold and mistrustful.

'When I've become familiar with French, I'll go to Paris and fend for myself. Maybe I'll become naturalized. Are you all naturalized?'

'Father was already French before the war. I did my military service in France.'

Hans didn't linger in Joseph's room but left him alone with his thesis on bilateral pneumothorax . . . *Thanks to fluoroscopy, it will be possible from the onset of bilateral pneumothorax to register the degree of pulmonary collapse and . . .*

These were the last words in the exercise book. Piano chords echoed through the house. Hans went and sat down behind his cousin Liesbeth, who had a long, sharp nose.

'Not much of a laugh, your brother, is he?'

She smiled but said nothing.

'Or your sister Anna for that matter!'

The wallpaper had a pattern of small flowers. Summer entered through the open window, along with the noises of the street and especially the bell of the yellow tram sounding triumphantly every three minutes. The stop was only fifty metres away, and every time a tram came to a halt, you heard the screech of the brakes, which caused a little sand to fall on the rails.

'Talking to your father earlier,' Hans said, looking at the back of his cousin's neck, 'I was quite embarrassed.'

'Why? Because Father almost never speaks?'

'No. Because he asked after my father.'

'And that was embarrassing?'

'Yes, it was. My father died fifteen years ago.'

He said this quite cheerfully, and Liesbeth, who turned abruptly to look at him, couldn't help smiling, too.

'What about his letter? The one he just wrote to my parents?'

'I wrote it!'

'Why?'

He scratched his head comically. Although he was the German Krull, as they called him here, he was almost dark, almost southern in appearance, while the French Krulls still had complexions like Danish porcelain.

'I'm not really sure. I thought a letter from my father would make more impression than a letter from me. I'm pretty good at imitating handwriting. So I wrote that my son Hans needed to spend two or three months in France to improve his French.'

He was looking her in the eyes, and she was the one forced to turn her head away.

'Are you angry?'

'It's none of my business. But what if my father . . . ?'

'Will you tell him?'

'What do you take me for?'

'You understand, I absolutely had to leave Germany and I was down to my last few marks. I thought of my father's brother, though I wasn't sure if he was still living in the same town after all these years. It seems odd to me, people staying so long in one place.'

'What about you?'

'I've lived all over Germany – Berlin, Munich – Austria, too, then in Hamburg and on a ship of the Hamburg America Line.'

'What did you do?'

'A bit of everything. On the ship, I was a musician. In Berlin, I was in the film business.'

'Best not to talk about that here,' she said, turning to her piano.

'I know!'

'So why have you told me on your first day?'

'No reason!' he replied, heading for the door and stopping for a moment to look her up and down.

Immediately afterwards, strings of notes emerged from the lounge.

It had been barely twenty-four hours, and Hans was moving about the house with as much ease as if he had spent his whole childhood there; he even, from wherever he was, recognized the voice of Pipi, who came ten times a day on errands for the bargees and each time had her little drink.

He had familiarized himself not only with the house, but with the surroundings. First of all, the town didn't count. They were right on the edge of it, barely part of it.

Proof of that was that less than fifty metres away the tram stopped, performed a manoeuvre and went back the way it had come.

Facing the house was the broad quayside, with three or four rows of trees, benches and beams, timber and bricks unloaded from the barges . . .

Beyond the canal, a kind of waste area or parade ground on which stood a long red building which was the army firing range; and there, from morning to evening, rifle shots could be heard like the cracking of whips. But that was on the other side of the water. It wasn't part of Quai Saint-Léonard and so didn't count.

On Quai Saint-Léonard, the only building after the Krull grocery was a house with an adjoining workshop: Guérin Carpenters.

Then, on the edge of the water, a large yard with dried-out barges and unfinished boats: Rideau Boat Builders.

'Don't you ever take a stroll along the canal?' Hans asked Liesbeth.

'They don't let me go out on my own.'

'So when do you ever go for a walk?'

'On Sundays, when the whole family goes to church.'

The French Krulls, like those in Emden, had remained staunch Protestants.

'Don't you ever get bored?'

'I'm always bored!'

He, on the other hand, wasn't. He nosed about the house, sniffing in every nook and cranny, finding everything amusing, even Anna and the seriousness with which she played her role.

'Will you take some cheese, cousin?'

'Why "take"? Why don't you say "eat"?'

'Because in French we say "take cheese". I take cheese, you take cheese . . .'

He never forgot anything she said and a few hours later, with a gleam in his eye, would kindly point out that she was contradicting herself. And from time to time, for no apparent reason, he would wink at Liesbeth, who would turn her head away.

Cornelius Krull, even after spending four-fifths of his life in France, still hadn't learned French. But he had almost forgotten his German, so that he spoke in a curious mixture that only his family could understand.

'Has Pipi been in again, Aunt Maria?'

Imposing as she was, he often teased his aunt.

'Why do you always keep both your hands on your belly?' he would ask her innocently.

Two days? Not even that! He had been there a day and a half, idle and nonchalant.

It was about eleven o'clock in the morning, an hour he loved because of the light, the kitchen smells, the constant ringing of the shop bell.

He had just gone upstairs to his room, without knowing quite why, after taking a piece of sausage from the cold store. He had stretched out fully clothed on his bed, listening. From the next room, he heard the recognizable sounds of Liesbeth turning over her mattress and putting the blanket back on.

Looking up at the ceiling, where the flies had left stippled marks, he seemed to be asking himself:

'How about it? Should I try? Or should I leave it?'

He chewed the last mouthful of sausage, stood up, wiped his lips and smiled at himself in the mirror. Then he very gently turned the door knob, stood listening on the landing, then grabbed the knob of another door and opened this one without the slightest noise.

Proof that he had not been mistaken was that Liesbeth turned abruptly, gave a start and couldn't help casting a frightened look about her.

What was she afraid of, if not that?

The bed hadn't been completely tucked in . . .

And she didn't have a dress on under her smock!

'What are you . . .?'

He smiled, winked and closed the door.

When he tiptoed out a quarter of an hour later, he had a long scratch on his face, but even more of a gleam in his eye. He didn't turn round, because he didn't want to be too horrible. He turned the door knob, gently, noiselessly, as only he could. And saw . . .

He saw Joseph standing there, not completely level with him, because he had walked down a few steps, and only the top part of his body was visible.

Joseph was pale, paler than usual, his features contracted in an unsettling way. He looked as if he were about to run away, as if he had been caught with his eye to the keyhole.

Hans didn't wonder for very long what he had to do. It was automatic. He simply winked and went back into his room, where he looked out of the window at a passing train, the green mass of the trees, light shimmering on the water between the trunks, and sniffed a little at the lingering smell of Liesbeth on his body.

At lunch, Joseph didn't say anything. He was just as boring as usual, just as imbued with the solemn nature of life.

Old Cornelius, who alone was entitled to a wicker armchair, never spoke. Hans had already wondered if it was because he was stupid.

It was Anna who dealt with Hans.

'What do you call this?' she asked, pointing to the dish.

'Carrots.'

'And this?'

'Meat!'

'Mutton chops. Repeat. Mutton . . .'

He would have liked to laugh and nudge Liesbeth, who was sitting next to him, with his elbow, even – why not? – ask her out loud:

'What do you call what we did earlier?'

He held back, keeping it all to himself. Strictly speaking, he wasn't smiling, but his whole being exuded cheerfulness.

'Aren't you eating, Liesbeth?' Aunt Maria scolded.

'I'm not hungry.'

He nevertheless amused himself by decreeing in a tone that would have suited the solemn Joseph:

'Young people your age should always be hungry!'

She threw him a sad glance. Seeing that her eyes had misted over, he gave her knee a joyful squeeze.

'Isn't that so, Joseph? You, being a doctor . . .'

There was no way the others could understand. They thought it was an ordinary day, filled with peace and sunshine. They had no idea that it had taken only a few minutes to . . .

Suddenly, Liesbeth stood up, her face buried in her table napkin, and walked out. They could hear her sobbing hoarsely.

'What's the matter with her?'

Joseph was looking his cousin in the eyes, Old Cornelius was chewing slowly, not thinking of anything else, while in the workshop, his assistant was gnawing at the packed lunch he brought every morning . . .

'How about going for a little walk, cousin?'

'Call him Joseph, Hans!' Aunt Maria cut in.

It was evening. The family were all sitting out on the pavement, their backs to the house, the uncle in his wicker armchair, the others on straw-bottomed chairs.

The sun had only just set. Moist, cool air rose from the canal, and thin strands of fog were starting to form between the trees.

Twenty metres further along the street, outside the carpenter's doorway, there were other chairs, other people, but these people had nothing to do with the Krulls and weren't looking their way.

Cornelius was smoking a long porcelain pipe, his eyes half-closed, his beard as stiff as that of a carved saint. Aunt Maria was sewing red cotton on the corners of a pile of check table napkins. Anna had brought out a book but wasn't reading it, and Liesbeth, claiming she wasn't feeling well, had gone to bed.

The world was almost empty. The barges were asleep. A thin jet of water filtered through a lock gate that hadn't been properly closed, making a sound like a fountain, interspersed every ten minutes by the din of the tram, although this grew less frequent as darkness wore on.

'Good idea. Go for a little walk. But don't come back too late.'

Hans never wore a hat, which accentuated his casual demeanour. He wore soft shirts with open collars, and his clothes had a particular looseness that underlined Joseph's stiffness.

Why did little circles endlessly appear on the smooth surface of the canal, as if bearing witness to an inner life?

The two young men strode slowly along.

They weren't just the same age, but the same height, and they both had long legs and large feet.

'You're not saying anything, Cousin Joseph!'

Turning, they could see the family, motionless on the threshold of the house, and the other family, the carpenter's, grouped a little further along the pavement. On one of the barges, washing was drying on lines.

'I'm wondering what you're planning to do with my sister.'

'I'm not planning to do anything!'

The edge of the town was behind them, and what lay ahead was already the country, or rather an in-between zone, with hedges, nettles and patches of waste ground, but no meadows or cows yet.

'Were you looking through the keyhole?' Hans asked casually.

He didn't turn to look at his cousin. It wasn't necessary to do so to know that Joseph was blushing.

'If you were, you must have noticed that she wanted it as much as I did.'

What he saw was Joseph's hand, a long hand, paler in the twilight, a strangely shaped hand that suddenly started shaking.

'Why did you come to our house?' Joseph asked in a hesitant voice.

'Because I didn't know where to go!'

'Why not somewhere else?'

'I've already told you. My father had just one brother and one sister. The sister's in a convent in Lübeck. I could hardly go there.'

And in a lighter tone:

'Did you do any work today?'

'No!'

'Because of that?'

'Because of everything.'

'Meaning what?'

'Meaning everything!'

His hands were still shaking. He had stopped less than twenty metres from a streetlamp, the last one before the definitive darkness of the countryside. Following the direction of his gaze, Hans made out a vague mass, a couple standing in the shadows, a man and a woman embracing, the woman up on tiptoe the better to glue her lips to her companion's.

'Who's that?' he asked, without attaching any importance to the question.

'Sidonie.'

'Who's Sidonie?'

'Pipi's daughter . . . It doesn't matter . . .'

'Tell me, Joseph!'

'What?'

'Aren't you all a little bit . . . a little bit strange in your family?'

It wasn't the right word. He had hesitated. If he had known the word 'eccentric', he would doubtless have chosen that.

'Why do you say that?'

'No reason. It's just that there are things I sometimes think about . . . My father's sister, your aunt, when she decided she didn't want to be a Lutheran any more, after reading some book or other, entered a convent, and some say she has visions . . . My father, for two years before he died, hadn't been able to stand the sight of the colour red. And do you know how he died?'

'My father's normal!' Joseph said resolutely.

'Quite possibly. I was talking for the sake of it . . . Are there always so many boats on the canal?'

'Always. It's the main harbour of the town.'

'Do you have a lot of friends?'

'I don't have any!'

'Not even at the university?'

'They don't like young men whose mothers serve drinks to carters.'

'Why does she do it?'

'Because the local people think of us as foreigners and don't come into our shop. Without the bargees and the carters . . .'

The path was nothing now but a narrow towpath alongside the canal. A small boat glided by, piloted by a poacher on his way to lay traps, who kept an eye on the banks as he sculled.

'Do you have a girlfriend, Cousin Joseph?'

'No.'

It was an unpleasant, bad-tempered 'no'.

'Shall we walk back?'

They again saw the couple not far from the streetlamp. It was as if their lips hadn't come unstuck since the previous time. Further on, the dried-out barges in the boat-builder's yard, the carpenter's family outside the first house, and at last the Krull family, with the wicker armchair, the white beard, the long porcelain pipe and Aunt Maria's check apron.

The air was blue, the strands of fog a lighter blue, everything was blue, the sky, the trees, the blue of night, and so, too, when they went back inside, was the transparent sign for Remy Starch.

Before opening the door of his room, Hans stopped on the landing. Hearing a noise that sounded like a muffled sob, he shrugged.

Then, once in bed, he was aware of footsteps below. It was Joseph, going round in circles in his room, with no thought of sleep.

2.

Before the event, the terrible discovery on the bank of the canal, there were three more ordinary days and a Sunday. Which is to say that Hans got to know everything, firstly because, even in bed, he heard the slightest scratching and guessed what it was, and secondly because he was everywhere, tirelessly, in the kitchen behind Anna, in the shop when his Aunt Maria was serving a drink to a carter or arguing with Pipi, in Liesbeth's room, where his cousin no longer dared venture, in the workshop and in Joseph's room; most often they hadn't seen him come in and would give a start when they did see him, wondering how long he had been watching them.

He had discovered that Cornelius was always the first up, and that it had been that way since the early days of his marriage. Perhaps it had been unintentional the first time, but then he had continued. He would go downstairs in his slippers, as noiseless as a mouse gnawing at something, and proceed to the cellar, where he would fill two buckets with coal. Then he would light the fire, as Hans knew from the whiff of petrol that came to him, because Cornelius sprinkled the wood with petrol.

Then the door of the shop would open; Cornelius would grind the coffee and finally, while waiting for the water to boil, would fill his long pipe.

At six, he would creep upstairs and place a cup of coffee on his wife's bedside table.

Hans also discovered . . .

Something he didn't yet know and that he learned that Sunday! Firstly, that although the shutters of the shop were closed, the door remained half open, and they not only sold groceries, but also served drinks. Secondly, that not everybody went to church, again because of the shop: Aunt Maria and Anna would take turns to stay behind.

That day, the others caught the tram at the corner of the street. Even just waiting at the stop had a certain solemnity about it. Cornelius in his frock coat, his hands stiff in grey cotton gloves, stared straight ahead. Joseph kept his bored air and had inherited from his mother the habit of tilting his head to one side in a nostalgic or resigned attitude.

God moves in mysterious ways . . .

That was the theme of the sermon that Sunday. By the time they left church, the town was bustling. In the central neighbourhood where they found themselves, the fair was in full swing.

'Have you ever been on a carousel, cousin?' Hans asked Liesbeth.

As soon as he looked at her, she felt obliged to blush, and Joseph was no better at sustaining his cousin's gaze.

Hans laughed, realizing how strange it was for the Krull family to be making their way through the crowd attending the fair. Not only had they just come out of a Protestant church rather than a Catholic one, not only did Uncle Cornelius barely speak French, but everything about them, even Joseph's resigned smile, was alien to the things that surrounded them.

Instead of catching the tram at the stop where they had got off, they went, by tradition, to the following stop and, again traditionally, dropped by a pastry shop to buy a cake, which Liesbeth carried by the string.

Poor Liesbeth! She could no longer bear to have people

looking at her and was really worked up about the insignificant event that had marked her flesh! The strange thing was that she was more upset by the fact that Hans had looked at her body, piece by piece so to speak, than by what he had done! And even now she would occasionally lift her hand instinctively to her chest, as if to make sure that her little pear-shaped breasts were not bare!

'God moves in mysterious ways,' Joseph told his mother, who liked to know the theme of the sermon.

Monsieur Schoof came at three, with Marguerite. Although Hans hadn't met them before, he was familiar with every detail of their lives. Monsieur Schoof was the family's only friend. Another German, who had come to France at about the same time as Krull and had become naturalized, he had opened a shop in Rue Saint-Léonard that sold butter and cheese.

He was small and round and pink, with eyes of forget-me-not blue and lips like a baby sucking at a bottle, and Marguerite was no less fresh, her plump body reminiscent of something edible.

She wasn't Joseph's fiancée, strictly speaking, but as good as: it had long ago been decided that they would marry.

Anna demonstrated a new crochet stitch; Marguerite blushed several times, whenever Hans' eyes readily came to rest on her blouse, which was full to bursting. What else did they do? Nothing. Cornelius said not a word. He sat there in his wicker armchair, as if posing for a family portrait, and only occasionally took his pipe out of his mouth with a hieratic gesture to mutter a few syllables to his friend Schoof.

Schoof was blissfully happy. They were both happy, out there on the pavement, looking at the canal, watching the tram passing from time to time, a family in their Sunday best paying a visit. The aroma of freshly prepared chocolate wafted from the carpenter's next door, where Sunday had much the same rhythm, and Hans would occasionally look at Joseph's hands, predicting the moment when they would tense in a spasm, as if his cousin suddenly felt dizzy.

'Shall we go upstairs for a while?' he whispered to Liesbeth, who was sitting quietly on her chair.

It would have been amusing, in this calm, with the window open and the family in a circle on the pavement, but Liesbeth recoiled as if someone had blasphemed in front of her.

How about with Anna? Unfortunately, she already had her mother's tough, solid appearance, and Hans had noticed that she wore a belt that made her look as hard as an old sideboard.

Time finally passed, since the table that had been cleared after lunch, laid for afternoon tea and then cleared again, was again covered in tablecloth and plates in anticipation of dinner.

Only after this last meal did Hans go out to roam about the fair, hatless as usual, his hands in his pockets, a cigarette between his lips, with that air of being at home everywhere that unsettled Joseph.

He noticed a young girl he was almost sure he recognized as the one he had seen in the shadows of the quayside, clinging to a man: Sidonic, daughter of the famous Pipi.

He followed her for a while through the crowd. She was arm in arm with another girl even younger than her. Although she was only sixteen, Sidonie was playing the young lady, or rather the elegant courtesan.

She must have seen *The Lady of the Camellias*, and she moved through the fair imagining she was the focus of all eyes, the girl who aroused all men's desire and all women's jealousy.

You sensed it from the way she walked, the way she looked about her, the way she leaned towards her meek companion and confided things in her with a laugh.

She wasn't ugly. She might have been thin, with a pale face, but she had finely drawn features and a nicely formed little body squeezed into an exaggeratedly tight suit tailored to emphasize her shapely young figure.

Hans almost . . . But no! He shrugged. He wasn't up to taking her and her friend to all the fairground booths before drawing her – perhaps! – into some dark corner.

He suddenly did an about-turn on seeing his cousin Joseph strolling amid the crowd, just like him, except that Joseph looked tense, staring straight ahead as if he were doing something very serious or very difficult.

Hans amused himself for a while, watching Joseph from a distance, and he was very pleased when he saw the tall, stern young man awkwardly following on the heels of Sidonie.

'I bet his fingers are shaking!' he thought.

The Schoofs had long since gone home. The Krulls were asleep. Hans had a glass of beer on a café terrace, looked around for his cousin and went home to bed. A slight noise in the next room told him that Liesbeth wasn't asleep, but he didn't feel up to joining her, especially as she would cry, and he would have to talk.

The noise of coal being shovelled in the cellar, then, quite a while later, the coffee grinder. Hans got out of bed, for no reason, and went downstairs in his pyjamas, perhaps with the idea of seeing his uncle at close quarters.

It was raining lightly and steadily, bringing out the greenery on the quayside, although it wouldn't last. Millions of moving circles appeared and disappeared on the smooth face of the canal. Workers were passing on their bicycles.

'Good morning, uncle!'

Uncle Cornelius looked at him curiously, not yet used to this young man, let alone to the idea that someone could go out to take the air in his pyjamas. But he didn't say anything. He never said anything. Perhaps he was a halfwit, perhaps a philosopher quietly living his own life, protected by an invisible shell.

Just opposite the house, a motor barge, large and brown with a rounded bow, was getting ready to leave. On deck, the bargee's wife was pushing on her pole to move the boat away from the canal bank while below, her husband was trying to start the diesel engine, from which a few puffs could occasionally be heard.

The engine wouldn't start. The lock gate was open. Other barges were waiting behind that one. The woman leaned into the hatch and said something to her husband in Flemish.

Despite the rain, Hans crossed the road, still in slippers and pyjamas, his body at ease, his movements free, his first cigarette of the day between his lips.

For a moment, his attention shifted to a group of soldiers just entering the firing range on the other side of the canal. Then he tried to make out what the man and the woman were saying in Flemish.

Turning, he could see the Krull house, the Krull shop and his uncle in the doorway, with his long, very German pipe.

Suddenly, eddies stirred the water, and thick smoke spurted from the exhaust pipe. The bargee came out on to the deck and ran to the helm.

'Hey, you!' Hans called to him.

The man turned and leaned over to see what the young man was pointing at in the water.

Hans had no idea what it was either: something white in the eddies, like a thick piece of linen. The nose of the barge was already advancing between the dripping walls of the lock. The bargee leaned further over, looking straight ahead because of the manoeuvre, then suddenly let out a cry and began gesticulating.

Their curiosity aroused, those on the bank – the lock-keeper, an angler, some waiting bargees – moved closer. The man pushed the white thing towards the bank with his hook, and it was only now that everyone could see it was a body, stark naked and deathly pale, whose head couldn't yet be seen because, being heavier, it was still underwater.

Before anything else, the boat had to get through the lock. From the bank, the angler tried to bring the body in with the thick end of his rod, but the bamboo was too light, and each time, instead of coming closer, the white thing retreated.

Four or five people stood watching, but then more came from the moored boats: a little boy, a woman breastfeeding a child, a gas company employee in his cap . . .

One of the bargees went back on board, jumped into his skiff and rowed it towards the body. Just then, someone asked Hans:

'What is it?'

He shrugged. Nobody had noticed that it had stopped raining and a slight mist was beginning to rise from the canal.

At first the man in the skiff tried to pull the body out with his hook – a somewhat sickening sight, with the iron hook jabbing into the flesh – but each time the body came loose.

He hesitated, not disgusted but a little embarrassed all the same. He glanced at the onlookers, as if to say:

'Oh, well, there's only one thing to do . . .'

He bent double, took the thing in his arms and lifted it, held it for a few moments out of the water like a strange dummy, then finally let it drop, streaming with water, into his skiff.

There had been time enough to see that it was a woman, or rather, a young girl. And now, on the bank, people were walking slowly, following the skiff, which would moor a little further on, where it was easier.

The body had been laid on the grass embankment and a piece of tarpaulin thrown over it. A policeman was standing beside it, listening to the onlookers' comments.

When Hans made up his mind to walk back across the road to the house, everyone instinctively watched him go, perhaps because he had discovered the thing, perhaps because he was in his pyjamas and spoke a foreign language.

Aunt Maria, who had just come down, was looking out through the shop window. Hans announced:

'They've fished up a body.'

'Bodies are brought up out of the water every month,' she replied. 'They always end up opposite our house. Anyone would think they do it deliberately.'

Hans' pyjamas were wet, and he felt a little cold; he went upstairs to his room to put on a jacket, but kept on his pyjama bottoms.

On his way back downstairs, he met his cousin Joseph, who, when he hadn't washed, had a face like blotting paper.

'What's going on?' he asked. 'Fished up another drowned man, have they?'

'A drowned girl!' Hans said.

'Oh!'

'I think it's Sidonie.'

There could be no doubt: Joseph's fingers were shaking. And at the same time, his Adam's apple almost leaped up in his thin neck.

'Who says that?'

'Nobody. Just me. By the way, cousin . . .'

'What?'

'Nothing!' Hans said, continuing on his way.

It was more practical. And besides, he had already wasted enough time and wanted to see what was going to happen next.

By the time he reached the bank, there was a crowd of at least fifty, and if you turned, you could see more people in the doorways and at the windows. A man who was still half asleep, without a false collar or a tie, arrived panting, led by a barefoot little boy.

He was the doctor. He looked at the onlookers reproach-fully, gestured for them to move aside, bent and lifted a corner of the tarpaulin.

Of course, he didn't need to touch the body, which was as dead as could be, but he turned to the policeman and said in a low voice:

'It's Sidonie Pipi.'

He had treated her on several occasions. In fact, as she was tubercular, he had even tried to get her into a sanatorium. But her mother, who didn't believe in doctors or illness, hadn't wanted her to go, especially as Sidonie, who worked as an assis-tant in a shoe shop, brought in a little money.

'Is the inspector coming?'

Again, he looked ill-humouredly at these people, who were all standing there gazing down at a tarpaulin. He would have to wait. The sky was no longer pale blue as it had been at first, but pink, with just a little blue in the distance. Opposite, the shooting was starting, each shot shaking the air. A boat's siren summoned the lock-keeper, who reluctantly moved away.

Hans was the only person who found it natural to be there in his pyjama bottoms, his torso naked under a greenish jacket. He didn't notice people looking at him and exchanging com-ments about him. He was waiting for Joseph, who finally crossed the road in the company of his sister Liesbeth.

Liesbeth looked at the little heap under the tarpaulin and asked:

'Is that it?'

She shuddered, drew her shawl across her chest and stam-mered as she walked away:

'I'd rather go . . .'

They were looking at Joseph, too, even though there was nothing unusual or preposterous in the way he was dressed. They were looking at him because he was the son of Cornelius Krull, and the Krulls were a clan apart.

He didn't say anything. He had merely nodded at the doctor. He was standing next to Hans and from time to time wiped the sweat off his upper lip with his finger.

The inspector arrived at last, on his bicycle. He didn't even bother to lift the tarpaulin but took the doctor aside, and they both walked up and down for a while, talking in low voices and gesticulating. After which, the inspector sent one of his men on an errand.

He himself, filling and lighting his pipe, walked along the bank in the direction of the boat-builder's yard, but went right past it. It became obvious that he was going to see Pipi.

Almost everyone followed, at a distance, of course. The first trams were running. Sirens and whistles announced that work was resuming in the factories and workshops.

Hans, who was walking with the crowd, wasn't surprised to see that Joseph was still by his side.

'She's probably drunk!' he said.

Pipi's barge wasn't a real barge of thirty-something metres, but a broken-down little Dutch boat, more than half of which rested on silt. To get on it, you had to cross an unsteady plank that made the inspector think twice.

Once on deck, he bent down and knocked at the hatch, waited, then bent down again and called.

At last Pipi's face appeared, swollen and distorted as it usually was in the morning, with big, expressionless eyes. They couldn't hear what the inspector said to her, and she disappeared for a few seconds, emerged again, first her upper body, then her legs, and rushed to the plank serving as a gangway, growling at the crowd:

'It's a terrible thing!'

But it wasn't clear what exactly was terrible: seeing people waste their time watching a spectacle like this or suddenly hearing that her daughter was dead.

Hans was struck by a small detail. As she walked, Pipi, who was breathing heavily, came very close to Joseph and paused for a moment, as if on the point of yelling at him. But her momentum took her past young Krull, and she continued on her way, talking to herself, while the crowd, including the inspector, kept following her at a distance.

Hans spotted his aunt and Anna in the doorway of the grocery but didn't see his uncle, or the assistant, or his cousin Liesbeth, who must have been in an awful state.

'Go on, show her to me!' Pipi screamed, as if challenging the crowd and the authorities.

What her face expressed when she glimpsed her daughter's face under the tarpaulin wasn't so much grief as hatred.

'It's a terrible thing!'

Her mouth twisted as if she was about to cry, but she didn't. She would have liked to do something. She felt it was necessary. She couldn't think what and she suddenly turned to the onlookers, raised her fist and cried:

'Aren't you ashamed to be watching this, you bunch of idlers? Think you're at the theatre, do you?'

The van from the morgue stopped just outside the Krull grocery. Two men crossed the road with a stretcher, and for a moment there was another glimpse of the pale body, on which the leaves of the plane trees cast dancing shadows.

Stunned, Pipi asked the inspector:

'Where are they going to take my poor girl now?'

She stank of alcohol. She was dirty. People stepped aside as she passed, afraid as much of fleas as of a torrent of abuse.

'Bring her to me!' the inspector said to one of the police officers.

He preferred to leave on his bicycle. The officer walked down the street with Pipi, seeming to lead her, and some people followed them all the way to the police station.

The doctor was off to one side, speaking to a local bigwig, and Hans caught the words:

'. . . post-mortem . . .'

He went back to the house and had breakfast mechanically, all alone in the kitchen. When he went upstairs to dress, Liesbeth's door was open. It was clearly deliberate. She was pretending to work, but her face was haggard, her eyes beseeching.

'It's horrible, Hans!' she moaned.

And her tears welled up and brimmed over, swelling her eyelids just as her lips swelled with sobs.

'Hans!'

It wasn't just Sidonie. It was everything. Her nerves, too . . . Didn't he realize that she needed to be reassured, to be clasped to his chest, to hear words, no matter which?

'True, it wasn't a pretty sight!' he admitted.

He wasn't moved by his cousin's tears, and reassuring her was a chore he was determined to avoid.

He went to his own room, closed the door, took off his jacket and filled his washbowl with water.

He was aware of her next door, still in a state. He sensed the sobs, the waving of the handkerchief, the grimaces and no doubt, despite everything, the occasional little glance in the mirror to see herself crying.

Then the swaying of a dress in the corridor, a silence, stillness, a rustle, a scratching at the door.

His shaving brush in his hand, he lathered his cheeks and his eyes sparkled with mischief.

'Hans . . .'

It was only a sigh. Nobody downstairs must hear.

'I'm very unhappy, Hans . . .'

Too bad! He had no desire to open the door and he almost went so far as to lock it.

It was Sidonie who had died, and yet it was Liesbeth who was unhappy!

The local newspaper only came out in the morning, so that it was necessary to wait until the next day to get the official news.

But well before that, everyone understood that something serious was going on. First, at eleven, a car stopped so close to the grocery that Aunt Maria gave a start, thinking that it was for her.

It was four dark-clad men from the prosecutor's office, who crossed the road to the canal bank, where the inspector was waiting for them.

The life of the harbour had long since got back to normal. There was the sound of shots from the firing range, the carpenters' hammers from the Rideau boatyard, the din of the lock every time it filled or emptied.

Yet within a few moments, a group had formed, more hesitant, more timid than in the morning, thanks to the prestige of these men.

Hans crossed the road, his hands in his pockets. Turning his head, he saw his cousin in his room, in shirtsleeves, bent over his exercise books.

'Who was the first to notice the body?' the examining magistrate asked. To which the inspector replied:

'The bargee from the *Belle Hélène*. I gave him permission to go on his way. I thought that would be all right, given that I took down his statement.'

Hans now stepped forwards. 'I'm the one who saw the body,' he asserted.

His accent and his bad French provoked frowns. They looked at each other as if to say:

'Where did this one spring from?'

'I was getting some fresh air. I live opposite, with my uncle, Cornelius Krull. I saw something near the barge's propeller.'

'Would you mind questioning him, inspector?'

'I'll summon him later.'

Hans kept standing there. They didn't know how to get rid of him.

'Thank you,' the examining magistrate said.

Hans moved away slightly but continued to eavesdrop.

'What does her mother say?'

'First, when she was in a real state, she claimed it was Potut.'

'Who's Potut?'

'The man she lives with, more or less as his wife. If you like, we can visit the barge later. Mind you, it's full of fleas and vermin. Just setting foot on deck, you're covered in them.'

'You were telling me about Potut.'

'He was respectable once, even had an education. I think he used to be a croupier. Now he's drunk all day long, just like her. In the mornings, he hangs around the vegetable market, looking to do the odd bit of work. Actually, she's the one who supports him.'

'Where is this Potut?'

'We don't know, but it won't take us long to find him. Sometimes he's away for two or three days, sleeping it off somewhere. He didn't come home last night. Then again, the fair is on in Sainte-Marguerite. He always manages to pick up the odd bit of work . . .'

The examining magistrate threw a stern look at Hans, who was all too obviously eavesdropping, but the young man didn't seem to notice and nonchalantly lit a cigarette.

'And the girl?'

'You have to realize, with the three of them living on top of each other . . . Apparently, Potut did try once. The barge only has one liveable room, if you can call it that . . .'

'Are we sure she was strangled?' the deputy prosecutor asked.

'Strangled and raped. Right here, probably, given the traces of grass they found on her. We need to find her clothes. Most likely, they're in the canal.'

'What about her shoes?' the examining magistrate asked.

'No, her shoes and stockings were left on.'

From time to time, Hans looked across the road and caught the rectangle of a window, shirtsleeves dazzling white in the semi-darkness, close-cropped hair above a thick exercise book.

'I'll get some men to drag the canal.'

'What have you done with Pipi?'

'Released her. She's probably getting drunk in some bistro or other. When she'd as good as accused Potut and I read her back her statement, she looked at me in astonishment, denied everything, swore she'd never said it and that Potut was incapable of hurting her daughter. You see what we're up against! When she's got a few drinks inside her, she'll probably come out with a whole other story . . .'

The examining magistrate was taking notes with a gold propelling pencil in a notebook as tiny and immaculate as a dance card.

He made up his mind. 'Let's take a look at the barge anyway.'

He turned towards Hans, blinked and said curtly:

'As for you, you'll be summoned to the police station for questioning if need be.'

That didn't stop Hans from joining a few others and following the men as they walked alongside the canal and hesitated when they saw the rickety plank leading to the barge.

'Couldn't we get hold of another gangway?' the deputy prosecutor suggested.

The inspector took it upon himself to negotiate with Rideau, the boat-builder. The men from the prosecutor's office were in no hurry. They smoked and looked at their surroundings.

'The curious thing,' the examining magistrate remarked,

cutting off the end of a cigar with his teeth, 'is that, according to the pathologist, this Sidonie was still a virgin before last night.'

And with this word, an ambiguous smile hovered over his lips.

'Really curious!' he repeated, striking a match. 'Don't you think?'

'What I find curious, if it happened on the canal bank, is that nobody heard anything. There were barges nearby. There are houses.'

'But if he immediately put his hands round her throat . . .'

'Do you think she knew her attacker?'

'Quite likely! She was probably walking with him.'

Near Hans, a young boy was listening intently. Less than five metres away, two even younger boys were rolling in the grass like puppies. A woman on one of the barges was doing her washing, which reminded Hans of Remy Starch and Reckitt's Laundry Blue.

To get in through the hatch, the men from the prosecutor's office rolled up their trouser legs and trod carefully, emitting little cries like young ladies afraid of dirtying themselves.

At that very moment, Pipi entered the Krull shop, her pupils already dilated, as usually only happened towards evening. She threw a harsh look at Aunt Maria, who was her sworn enemy, and said by way of greeting:

'Dirty old bitch!'

She went straight to the zinc area at the end of the counter and grunted:

'So, are you going to serve me?'

Aunt Maria sighed and grabbed a bottle of rum with a kind of tin spout that opened as soon as the bottle was tilted.

'My poor Pipi . . .'

'I don't need anyone to feel sorry for me.'

'Now you see where it all leads . . .'

Perhaps Pipi was as necessary to Aunt Maria as Aunt Maria was to Pipi. One of them could come there regularly to unload her bitterness, finding in the Krull shop a place where, while drinking, she was at liberty to focus all her hates and resentments.

Aunt Maria, for her part, was able, from a position of great virtue, to sigh over a perfect specimen of human degeneration.

'You should be ashamed of yourself, drinking on a day like today!'

To which Pipi, already drunk, retorted:

'When should I drink, then? If your daughter had been raped and murdered . . .'

And all at once she burst into tears.

3.

Between the time Sidonie died and was thrown naked into the canal and the time when people started to take an interest in her, no longer as a poor, sickly young girl but as one of the elements in a drama that was bigger than her, at least ten days passed; ten days during which, all things considered, there was no Sidonie at all, neither the flesh and blood one who had died nor the other who was not yet born.

Nobody was doing it deliberately. She wasn't being ostracized. The inspector and the prosecutor's office had visited the scene of the crime, and a small crowd had followed their movements along the canal.

The following morning, it was in perfectly good faith that the newspaper was to write, on its local news page, which was never well printed:

Saint-Léonard neighbourhood. Bargees pulled out of the canal, near the lock, the body of one Sidonie S—, a shop assistant, who seems to have spent a night in the water. According to the post-mortem, before being thrown in the canal, Sidonie S— was subjected to an appalling assault and strangled. An investigation has been launched.

Much further on, two lines without a headline:

The police have arrested one Potut, suspected of being the perpetrator of the appalling attack on Quai Saint-Léonard. Potut was too drunk to be interrogated meaningfully.

It should be added that the following days were particularly hot. As happened every summer, the water in the canal began to smell. Fly papers had to be put in every corner and within a few minutes were covered in a thick black layer of buzzing flies.

There were also prize-givings in the schools. And also a ridiculous little merry-go-round, a merry-go-round for children, pushed by a pony, which was set up next to the Rideau boatyard, perhaps because there was nowhere else for it to go during the holidays; from time to time, the owner would set it in motion, and its shrill music could be heard from as far away as the lock.

Even if they had asked Aunt Maria, who tended to have premonitions about many things, she would probably have asserted that there would never be a 'Sidonie case'.

The proof of this was that the very day the body had been discovered, she already had other concerns. The window display in the shop came up to her eyes, which meant that by standing upright, without needing to get up on tiptoe, she could see what was happening outside.

Passers-by who stopped in front of the shop window sometimes jumped on suddenly discovering the top of that head, those eyes, that forehead, that silver hair in the calm semidarkness of the shop. Some went away embarrassed, or annoyed, as if they had been caught off guard.

That day, Aunt Maria was looking further, over towards the canal bank, where figures bustled about and onlookers followed the efforts of men in two small boats.

These men had been given the task of dragging the canal for Sidonie's clothes.

But what concerned Maria Krull, what irritated her, was Hans, who was going from group to group and holding forth. He was all the more easily recognizable in that he was dressed in light grey, without a hat, the collar of his shirt open, and always with that excessively casual and nonchalant air of his.

As his French was still elementary and his accent terrible, he was obliged, in order to make himself understood, to use big, sweeping gestures. Aunt Maria was losing patience.

'Someone absolutely must tell him,' she murmured to Anna, opening the door to the kitchen.

Anna wasn't allowed in the shop, any more than Liesbeth was, because it wasn't seemly for young girls to serve drinks.

It was Aunt Maria's domain. Even the most insolent of drunks didn't faze her, and she would throw them out like a man. Anna ruled over the kitchen, but between customers her mother would half open the door with its guipure curtain.

That day, she opened it more often than usual, gradually building up a genuine conversation which, from sentence to sentence, from sigh to sigh, filled almost the whole day.

'People already blame us for being foreigners! . . . If only he didn't get involved in everything that happens . . .'

It was the day for cleaning the knives and the silver, which Anna rubbed with a pink paste that gave off a sour smell.

Aunt Maria came and went, passing from the smell of the shop to that of the paste and the soup, always calm even though anxious, her hands flat on her belly.

'We should tell him not to talk to the neighbours. In town, it doesn't matter. He can see whoever he likes there. But here, in the neighbourhood . . . I'm sure he tells everyone he's German . . .'

Maria tilted her head to the right: she had suffered for so many years from being German that she had lost count.

Then the bell would ring, and she could be heard on the other side of the door, sighing again, because her female customers almost all had the habit of being unhappy, and Aunt Maria would share their complaints.

'You should give him sugared water once an hour,' she would recommend a bargee's wife carrying a baby who was literally green. 'When I had my third . . .'

Her forehead peeked out through the window, her white hair, her eyes, and when she again opened the kitchen door it was to exclaim:

'Jesus, Mary and Joseph! Do you know what he's doing now? He's in a boat with those men, helping them to drag the canal!'

'I don't like him!' Anna had declared once and for all.

In saying this, her eyes were heavy, heavy with resentment, with secret thoughts.

Joseph was working upstairs. He had been working far too much for some time now, and, whenever he came downstairs for meals, his complexion was like papier mâché, his eyes so tired that the eyelids flickered constantly like those of birds dazzled by the light.

'You should get some air.'

'I'll have plenty of time for air once I've presented my thesis.'

He was like his mother, always sorrowful, always dignified and resigned, seeming to proclaim like Job:

'The Lord gave and the Lord hath taken away; blessed be the name of the Lord!'

When he came down for dinner that evening, he knew something was happening from his mother's more hermetic silence, his sister Anna's expression, his cousin Hans' slightly forced gusto.

It was Hans who said:

'They finally fished out the clothes. They were literally torn to pieces.'

His aunt coughed and indicated Liesbeth with a look, which Hans didn't understand immediately. When he did, he concealed his smile behind a pout.

So they didn't talk about Sidonie. They didn't talk about anything, really – just the heat, which, if it continued, might hinder traffic on the canal, as it had two years earlier, when the water had been too low for a whole month.

As they left the table, there was something indefinable in Aunt Maria's attitude, something comprehensible only to the Krulls, something that said:

'Don't go too far. Let Hans leave. We have to talk.'

That made Hans, who had a sixth sense, all the more cheerful. Nevertheless, he decided to go out, announcing:

'I'm going to town, but I'll be back . . .'

Maria Krull, unable to stay idle, was peeling potatoes. They didn't switch the lights on. In summer, they liked to remain in semi-darkness until it was impossible to see anything. Even if they didn't sit outside, the shop door and the kitchen door were left open, so that they had a constant view of the canal and the dark-green trees.

'Listen, Joseph. Maybe you should talk to him . . . No, stay!'

Joseph had been on the verge of going upstairs to his room and getting back to his exercise books.

'Just now, he came to see me in the shop. He didn't seem at all embarrassed. He asked me if I had any small change.'

Old Krull was sitting in his armchair, haloed by the twilight and the thin smoke from his pipe, holding his eyelids in such a way that it was impossible to make out if his eyes were open or closed.

'I thought it was because he didn't want to go upstairs and get his wallet. I asked him how much he wanted, and he said: "Give me a hundred francs . . ."'

Liesbeth left the room for no reason: it wasn't time for her piano lesson, and they had no idea where she was going to hide herself away.

'Then,' Maria Krull continued, her monologue interspersed by the sound of potatoes falling into the bucket, 'he told me he hadn't been able to get his money out of Germany, that the customs officers were very strict, that he could have been sent to prison or a concentration camp. What do you think, Joseph?'

'I don't know . . .'

He stood there, so tall that it looked as if he might not be able to get through the door.

'Has he told you how long he's planning to stay with us?'

'He hasn't mentioned it to me.'

'You should try and worm it out of him. He strikes me as so inconsiderate! Do you think he's a scrounger?'

In Maria Krull's mouth the word 'scrounger' meant something very particular, encompassing the notions of indecency, bad manners and dishonesty.

'People already think badly of us!'

'You're exaggerating, Mother!' Joseph said without conviction.

'Have you ever seen any of our neighbours come into the shop for anything? They prefer going an extra five hundred metres to another grocery.'

It was very characteristic of her. She wasn't crying. She never cried. But often, in the evening, when she let her thoughts take over, she would assume a monotonous, complaining tone, and as you couldn't see her eyes, you might assume they were wet.

'I really think you should talk to him, Joseph!'

'No, Mother. You're the one who should talk to him.'

'Anyone would think you're all scared of him!' Anna muttered.

There was nothing more in the newspaper about Sidonie. Even in the neighbourhood, people hardly mentioned her, firstly because Potut had been arrested and the mystery solved, secondly because everyone had children and it was best not to talk about such things in front of them.

Even the police inspector didn't think there was a 'Sidonie case'!

They had brought in Potut after finding him blind drunk in the station waiting room, where he often spent the night.

It wasn't until the following day that the inspector had had the man brought to his office and asked him point-blank:

'What were you doing the day before yesterday?'

The former croupier was a strange mixture of stupefaction and sharpness, or more precisely, even though he was most often in a stupor, shifting from one leg to another, a clear, sharp look would suddenly appear in his eyes, which was quite unsettling.

'Well, are you going to tell me what you were doing?'

He was shown a photograph of Sidonie's body, taken in the morgue: definitely not a pretty sight.

'Who's that?'

Potut needed glasses to see clearly. He had a pair, with dirty lenses, in his pocket, mixed up with cigarette ends, pieces of paper and string, and all sorts of other things.

When he recognized Sidonie, he simply said:

'Well, well . . .'

Then he repeated four or five times:

'Well, well . . . well, well . . .'

'Aren't you ashamed, you dirty old man? Did you really need to strangle her on top of everything else?'

The inspector puffed at his pipe. He was in no hurry. He turned from time to time towards his secretary and gave him a wink.

'What night was that?' Potut asked.

'Sunday. Don't pretend you don't know.'

'What if I told you where I was on Sunday night?'

'Oh, of course! You have an alibi.'

'I was with that fellow from Marseille!'

'What fellow from Marseille?'

'I don't know him. I'd seen him once or twice around Les Abbesses. He's an educated man, someone you can talk to.'

Little by little, Potut told his story. They had met on a bench on Sunday evening. This fellow from Marseille, a shabby tramp, was eating a piece of bread he'd been given by some people living in a caravan.

'Are you thirsty?' Potut had asked him.

'Why, do you have money?' the other man had replied.

'If the wife's not at home, I may find some under the mattress.'

Thick as thieves, they had made their way to the canal, where Potut had made his new friend stay behind while, as resourceful as a little boy, he had slipped on to the barge. Pipi was already asleep, so fast asleep that he had managed to take the thirty-six francs remaining under the mattress.

'Three ten-franc coins, one of five and one of one!' he specified.

Then they had gone on a drinking spree. They had walked the streets on their unsteady legs, dragging their feet. Potut had ended up at the railway station, he didn't remember how.

'Well, we'll see if we can find this fellow from Marseille. I'd be very surprised if we do.'

'I can even tell you what we talked about!'

'I'm not interested in that. It won't keep you out of prison.'

Twice in twenty-four hours, Pipi was arrested because she was drinking more than ever and when she was drunk, she took it out on the police, cursing them and blaming them for letting her daughter be raped.

The nights were almost as hot as the days and all the windows in the neighbourhood were kept open, with the result that as you passed in the street you had the impression you could hear people tossing and turning in their beds, sweaty and uncomfortable, attacked by mosquitoes.

It was on the Tuesday morning that Hans, who was going around in circles in the house, suddenly sat down astride a chair opposite his cousin Anna.

Liesbeth had gone out to her piano lesson. For two days now, Hans hadn't had a chance to be alone with her, and whenever she was in her room she kept the door locked.

Sometimes, Hans opened the door to Joseph's room, always finding his cousin determinedly buried in his work. Joseph would raise his eyes wearily, then pick up his pen again, carefully avoiding all conversation.

'Someone should tell him not to keep disturbing Joseph!' Aunt Maria had sighed during one of her appearances in the kitchen.

Someone should tell him . . .

It was becoming a refrain. There were lots of things to tell Hans, but nobody did. They were all content with talking behind his back.

It was irritating to know that he was in the house, at a loose end, nosing everywhere, sitting down here or there, humming German songs, or coming into the shop, even when there were female customers.

'But I try to make him see . . .' Aunt Maria would say.

He didn't see, or didn't want to, his demeanour as cheerful as ever.

'So, Cousin Anna, still glum?'

That morning, she was scrubbing the stove, her hair tied at the back with a handkerchief, her face spattered, her mood all the more aggressive.

'I'm not glum!'

'Don't tell me you're happy.'

'Do you think life is happy?'

'Oh, for God's sake!'

'It's obvious you haven't been living in this house since you were born!'

'That's just it! I've never known a more appealing house.'

She threw him a brief glance, thinking he was making fun of her.

He wasn't! Or if he was, he was hiding it perfectly.

'It's so pleasant. Everything's pleasant. And warm! And so quiet!'

Aunt Maria came in, sighed when she saw Hans, opened her mouth but closed it again without saying a word.

Only Uncle Cornelius' assistant laughed at Hans' jokes and listened to the stories he would come and tell him as he peeled strands of wicker.

No Sidonie . . . No 'Sidonie case' . . . But, in the house, there was a 'Hans case'.

'If he asks me for money again . . .'

'I hope we're not going to support him!'

'Someone really should tell him . . .'

But nobody did! And the most annoying thing was that they had the impression that he knew, that he guessed at all these little mysteries they were weaving around him.

Liesbeth's nose had never seemed so sharp. She hardly ate. When this was pointed out to her, she blamed the heat, and Hans would look at her with a mischievous gleam in his eye.

Until Wednesday evening . . . Everyone was going to bed, and old Krull, with that gesture straight out of a stained-glass window, traced a little cross on each person's forehead with his thumb.

Starting up the stairs, Hans said to Liesbeth under his breath:

'See you later, in my room . . .'

He left his window open, leaned there on his elbows and smoked a cigarette, hearing the others undressing in the other bedrooms.

Joseph wasn't asleep, hadn't gone to bed: leaning out, Hans could see a halo of light at his window. There was nobody on the quayside, and the stillness of the barges on the black, somehow eternal water was almost dramatic.

Suddenly Hans turned. He hadn't heard the door open or close, he hadn't been aware of any footsteps, but he wasn't too surprised to see Liesbeth standing rigidly behind him.

Her unlit face was pale, her eyes big and feverish as she looked at him. For a moment he felt as if he were in the presence of a sleepwalker.

'Come and sit down, Liesbeth,' he whispered, drawing her to the edge of the bed.

She remained stiff, but didn't resist.

'I'm really pleased you came. I thought maybe you were angry with me.'

This was the hardest part. His cousin's icy body had to be warmed up, and all the thoughts she had crammed into her little head for several days had to be dispelled.

'Come closer . . .'

'Listen, Hans, I came to have a serious talk . . .'

'Shh!'

Firstly, they could be heard. Secondly, he had no desire for a serious talk.

'I don't know what you have in mind, but if you left me alone now . . .'

Then two things happened at the same time, on different levels, and Hans managed to stay attentive to both.

Firstly, Liesbeth, clinging to him with incredible vigour, burst into sobs so loud that you might have thought the whole household would hear them.

He wasn't worried about that. It was perfectly fine. He just had to let her weep in his arms and stroke her gently.

But at the same time, there was a characteristic creaking on the floor below, the creaking of a door being opened cautiously. And by now Hans knew what that meant: Joseph, whose room it was, had heard noises and must already be climbing the stairs in the dark, taking care not to make a sound. In a few moments, he would be listening at the door or peering through the keyhole.

'You're a sweet girl, my poor Liesbeth . . . I like you a lot . . .'

He was whispering in her ear, knowing that, even though she was still crying, she could hear everything he said and was waiting for what would happen next.

'Really, a lot. But we have to be sensible. There's no point crying like this. We have to . . .'

It was still too early. He contented himself with stroking her forehead and cheeks, then put his cheek against hers.

There was another outburst, a few moments later, when Liesbeth abruptly clung to him even more strongly than before, saying:

'If you leave without me, I'll kill myself. I can't live in this house any more.'

'Then we'll leave together . . .'

He never made a tragedy out of things. He seemed to be cradling a feverish child, which didn't stop his hands from now caressing his cousin's body.

'When?'

'One day . . . Soon . . .'

Joseph was there, on the other side of the door! Hans never stopped thinking about it. And he said to himself:

'Provided he stays!'

Because it would still take a little time, half an hour or an hour.

The room was in shadow, and the sky seemed to enter through the wide-open window, with, in the distance, the voices of frogs and a train puffing in a station, as if undecided whether or not to leave.

'Shhh! Not another word, little cousin . . .'

He was the one talking, babbling on, whispering nonsense in her ear. It all took a little more than half an hour, but less than an hour.

Liesbeth went quite stiff, because it still frightened her, and her nostrils contracted.

'Shhh, my little Liesbeth . . . The two of us, just like that . . .'

He could almost hear Joseph breathing out on the landing. What he did hear clearly was Aunt Maria turning over in her bed and heaving a sigh, the sigh of a large woman unable to find a comfortable position.

'You won't cry again, will you, Liesbeth? Ever again?'

She didn't know. She was looking at him with a mixture of adoration and anguish. From time to time, her lower lip still quivered. If she had cried, she wouldn't have been able to say if it was from distress or joy.

He was smiling. It was a complicated smile, which both surprised her and worried her, and he explained in a casual tone:

'I'm thinking of your sister Anna doing what we're doing. Don't you think it'd be funny, Anna in this position?'

She tried to smile, too, but her eyes misted over. She didn't understand. She was confused, ashamed of her bare belly, which looked pale in the darkness. Her hands reached out to cling to Hans. It seemed to her that she was descending into an abyss of painful joy and despair.

'I'd like to see that!'

'See what?'

'Your sister . . . Shhh! If you cry . . .'

At such moments, Hans' eyes became so tender, so imploring, so full of gaiety and youth that Liesbeth panted a few more times, calmed down and resumed her regular breathing, a wan smile on her face.

*

Nobody even bothered to find out where and when Sidonie had been buried. Not even her mother!

Children in their Sunday best paraded with their prizes, surrounded by parents even stiffer than them. Liesbeth resumed playing the piano all day long and started eating again. As for Joseph, he now got into the habit of locking his door when he was working and was no longer seen speaking to his cousin.

'Don't you think he'll assume you're angry with him?'

'I don't care!'

'What have you got against him?'

'Nothing!'

'He is your father's nephew after all . . .'

Anna was turning sly, observing her sister with a little too much attention.

As for Potut, he was kept in prison until Saturday morning without even being questioned.

From time to time, the inspector would get a phone call from the examining magistrate, who was getting ready to leave for his holiday.

'Have you found him yet?'

It was only on Saturday morning, at the market, that the man from Marseille was spotted sitting calmly on a bench, eating a hot sausage. He was taken to the police station and asked what he had been doing for the past week. As calmly as could be, he said he had been in the country.

He would often leave, just like that, and come back. He didn't understand what the police wanted with him, given that his papers were in order.

'And Potut?'

'What about Potut?'

They had assumed they were home and dry. They had a feasible culprit. And now, in spite of the inspector's tricks, this fellow from Marseille confirmed everything Potut had said.

'If you ask at Léonie's, they'll tell you I broke a glass and they threw us out . . .'

It was a little bar behind the cathedral. Léonie also confirmed what the man had said, and at eleven they had no choice but to summon Potut to the examining magistrate's office.

'Sign this!'

'What is it? I left my glasses in the cell.'

'Your statement.'

'What are you going to do with me now?'

'You're free to go!'

Done! They put him outside, in the blazing sun, where he was suddenly disorientated. They didn't mention the man from Marseille, and as the latter had been released an hour earlier, they didn't have the good fortune to meet again.

It was increasingly hot. Potut talked to himself as he hugged the buildings, looking with surprise at a kind old lady who slipped a couple of sous in his hand as she passed.

As nobody was talking about Sidonie any more, there was no point telling the editors of the newspaper that they had had to release the only suspect, which meant that the people of the Saint-Léonard neighbourhood, there at the edge of the town, were surprised to see Potut hanging around the lock as he always had done.

Some claimed that there was a scene between him and Pipi, that they exchanged both insults and blows.

Only Hans could have told the truth, because he hadn't stopped prowling around the barge. It was that same evening, at the fair, that he triggered the 'Sidonie case', perhaps unwittingly, perhaps maliciously.

It was the penultimate day of the fair. There were going to be fireworks. This time, Hans hadn't asked Aunt Maria for money, he had asked Liesbeth, and she had given him the eighty francs she had in her handbag.

'Tonight . . .' he had promised her.

She would come! She would wait for him as long as she had to! And, for a half hour, a quarter of an hour of tenderness, lying motionless in his arms, listening to him whispering, she would accept whatever fantasy he came up with.

She didn't even dare protest when he said with a disquieting curl of the lips:

'You'll see! One of these days, we'll arrange it so that Anna . . .'

When she was alone, Liesbeth hardly dared touch her own body, and when she was with the others, she almost felt ashamed. But at night, for that quarter of an hour, for that half hour, with the window open on darkness . . .

With those eighty francs in his pocket, he was making his way through the crowd, past the fairground booths, when he spotted a strange little thing, a kind of monster, a girl of fifteen already as well shaped as a woman, with short legs, an arched back and a provocative chest.

He didn't know her name but he recognized her as the girl who had been with Sidonie the previous Saturday. Her friend being dead, she had a lanky girl with her, younger than she was, and both were laughing and showing off to the men around them.

'Good evening, ladies,' Hans said, as ceremonious as he was ironic.

'Monsieur?'

They played along with him, immediately convinced that he was going to flirt with them. The younger one pinched her companion's arm.

'Would you allow me to buy you drinks?'

'I don't know if . . .'

They were quivering with joy at being accosted like real women.

4.

'If it's all the same to you, I'd rather go to Victor's.'

They had moved away from the crowd and come to an ordinary-looking café terrace at the corner of a street, where Hans had suggested they sit. The girl-woman had pointed a bit further along the narrow, badly paved street to a lighted globe, beneath which the motionless figure of a policeman could be seen.

Victor's was a dance hall, and Hans' companion, thinking he was having second thoughts, hastened to say:

'It's no more expensive than anywhere else!'

She was staggeringly self-confident and composed. Like Sidonie, she was playing a role, or rather, she was having a waking dream, but it was neither the same role nor the same dream.

Sidonie had seen herself draped in lace and silk, or even an ermine cape, her skin translucent, her eyes nostalgic and distant, and she couldn't have had to make much of an effort, when the fairground crowd turned to look at her, to imagine young noblemen in tails.

This other girl, who was dumpy, with swollen breasts and buttocks just asking to be slapped, had pitched her ideal a few degrees lower in the hierarchy of seduction.

She was playing the worldly-wise girl of the people, a girl with her head screwed on, someone who, although capable of tender feelings, wasn't born yesterday.

The lighting in the dance hall was purple, which distorted the faces of the women. All you could see were eyes with dark rings under them, blueish cheeks and white lips, and Hans' companion underwent this transformation like the others.

'Hello, Victor!' she cried, passing the counter.

Victor almost didn't notice her, but when he did, said as if bestowing alms:

'Good evening, Germaine.'

The other girl, the younger one, made her way fearfully through this atmosphere bristling with accordion music, occasionally looking Hans up and down.

'Shall we sit here?'

'If you wish, Mademoiselle Germaine.'

'How do you know my name?'

He had just heard it, there was nothing clever about it! She knew that. It made a good impression, all the same.

'What will you have?'

'A mint lemonade. With a lot of mint! What about you, Ninie?'

'I'll have the same!'

Ninie was overawed. Like a child, she couldn't take her eyes off Hans. Lips half open, she gradually assumed a dumbfounded expression.

'You're foreign, aren't you?' Germaine simpered, powdering her face: a pointless activity in this lighting.

To which he replied, simply or cynically:

'German . . .'

That gave Ninie a little shock, and her eyes opened a bit wider. As for the plump Germaine, she said sententiously, like someone who knows what she is talking about:

'Oh! Just like the Krulls!'

Couples were dancing with expressionless faces, occasionally glancing at the mirrors on the walls. Ninie's legs, as she sat on the banquette, didn't reach the floor. She sucked at the straw she had been given. Did Hans frighten her just a little?

He wasn't like anyone she knew. Not in any way! First of all, he wasn't 'someone from the street', he went about without a hat, in an open-necked shirt – and it wasn't the kind of shirt that men wore in the country or at sea.

His square shoes were almost slippers, so soft you didn't hear him walking.

He wasn't a student. Nor was he a worker, or a young man like those who deliberately wore their caps at an angle.

'Fancy a dance?' Germaine suggested when she couldn't find anything to say.

He was twice as tall as her. He had to stoop. You expected to see him lift her off the ground. In spite of that, he wasn't ridiculous, nor was he embarrassed. Ninie watched the couple move around the room.

'You dance well, but you don't dance like the people here,' Germaine commented, resuming her seat.

'Do you often come to Victor's?'

'On Sunday afternoons. Sunday evenings, too, sometimes . . .'

People were looking at them. Everyone had noticed Hans, and there was a touch of contempt in their eyes, because he was with two such young girls. He wasn't the least bit affected by it.

'Did you come here with Sidonie?'

She was surprised, and there was a hint of suspicion in the look she gave him.

'Did you know Sidonie?'

'I heard about her.'

'Who from?'

'Friends.'

'What friends? I knew all Sidonie's friends. We were pretty much inseparable.'

She had already learned how to sigh solemnly to indicate her grief. She dabbed at the corners of her eyes with her hand-kerchief and said, in the tone of a precocious child imitating grown-ups:

'It's really awful!'

'Did she have lots of boyfriends?'

Little Ninie touched her friend's arm. Germaine, uncon-cerned with the unlikelihood of it – given that Hans was German – asked:

'You're not police, by any chance?'

Javas followed waltzes, and the same figures, the same waxen faces, glided around in the unreal light.

'I swear I'm not from the police. But I was near the canal when they took the body out.'

Germaine shuddered. Ninie looked around to make sure she wasn't in any danger, then, for further reassurance, took a big gulp of her mint lemonade.

'I thought someone might have followed the two of you last Sunday.'

It was too late to take back this unfortunate sentence, which would set it all off. Hans clearly sensed a barely perceptible shock in Germaine.

From one second to the next, she stopped being a young girl proud of strutting about in a dance hall with a man. A thought had struck her. She stopped looking him directly in the face.

'Why are you asking me all these questions?' she said. She wasn't playing a role any more, wasn't listening to the sound of her own voice.

Ninie touched her arm again and whispered:

'Let's go!'

'That's why you accosted us in the street, isn't it?'

The thoughts were coming thick and fast now. She was breathing heavily, her chest heaving.

'We have to go . . .'

'Why the hurry all of a sudden?' Hans said mockingly.

That was when she uttered the words:

'You're one of the Krulls, I bet! I should have noticed you look like the doctor.'

The local people already called Joseph the doctor.

With that, the two girls literally ran away, after each stammering:

'Goodbye, monsieur.'

When Hans got to the top of the stairs in the sleeping house, he stopped for a moment and, hearing nothing, touched Liesbeth's door. It swung open on to the darkness of the room; Liesbeth was standing by the door in her nightdress, barefoot, waiting.

He went in, walked over to the window and leaned his elbows on it. His cousin came and joined him. The rising moon illumined both of them, adding a greater sense of mystery to these two creatures motionless in the dark, framed in the window as if it were a picture hung on the side of the house.

Liesbeth had slipped her icy fingers into Hans' hand. She was waiting for whatever share of tenderness he might see fit to give her but didn't dare look at him for fear of seeing a bored or weary expression on his face.

But tonight Hans did not push away her cold hand. Instead, he put his arm round her shoulders, while still gazing out at the canal beyond the boatyard, where the beginning of the long line of poplars glowed silver in the moonlight.

'Do you also think I look like Joseph?' he asked under his breath.

'Who told you that?'

'It doesn't matter! What do you think?'

'Not at all! The two of you are quite different.'

'That's good!' was all he said in reply.

Without thinking, he was stroking one of her breasts through the thin material of her nightdress, and it took her a long time before she dared to sigh:

'You're hurting me.'

She was at one and the same time happy and anxious. He had never before been the way he was tonight: dreamy, as it were, almost tender. After a long silence, she huddled closer to him and ventured:

'When are we leaving?'

He didn't know if Joseph was behind the door or not. He hadn't listened out for those revealing little creaks. And now he was looking at Liesbeth, her sharp nose, her eyes that were always full of anguish when they came to rest on him.

'Come . . .'

He lay down on the bed, fully dressed, and let her lie down next to him and snuggle up against him. She didn't know if his eyes were open or closed, but she could hear his regular breathing, even the throbbing of his heart against her ear.

She was avoiding the slightest movement, almost stopping herself from breathing, so afraid was she of disturbing this state of things even a little. At last she heard a longer, deeper breath and felt his limbs relax.

He had fallen asleep, on her bed, and still she didn't move. She listened out for his heartbeat, held his wool-clad shoulder in both hands.

When she abruptly opened her eyes, day was breaking. She leaped off the bed, amazed that Hans was still there, asleep, a fine layer of sweat on his forehead and upper lip.

It was very early in the morning. On the canal, the barges hadn't yet got going. A carter was leading his horse along the quayside, with the harness and the ropes, but without the wagon.

'Hans . . .'

She touched him, almost timidly. When he opened his eyes, she was shivering. He raised his wrist to look at the time on his watch, yawned and moved first one leg, then the other off the bed.

He almost went back to his room without kissing her. He thought of it as he was already by the door and retraced his steps.

'See you later,' he murmured, his gaze elsewhere.

That morning, while all the family were having breakfast in the kitchen, he was more pensive than usual and kept looking at Joseph, who hadn't yet washed.

Apart from the fact that they were both very tall, there wasn't the slightest physical resemblance between them: not the shape of the face, not the complexion, not the eyes . . .

And yet that girl had detected a family likeness, and Hans was realizing that she was right!

His father, too, resembled old Cornelius, minus the beard, but then they were brothers.

That day, Liesbeth seemed a happy, healthy young girl, while Joseph, who didn't look at anybody, ate quickly, without pleasure, and went up to his room immediately afterwards.

For an hour, nothing happened. Hans went to get cigarettes from a shop 300 metres from the house and on the way back stood for a long time watching the lock in operation. Meanwhile, between customers, Aunt Maria had come and said to Anna:

'Do you think Liesbeth might be falling in love?'

'Who with?'

'Him!'

'I hope not, for her sake!'

'There are moments when he scares me. He has a way of looking at each of us in turn . . .'

She was interrupted by the shop bell and found herself face to face with Pipi.

'Give me something to drink, old girl!' sighed Sidonie's mother, who was in one of her self-pitying periods.

It was always one thing or the other with her. Either she would be aggressive and insulting or she would grab the first person she met and cry on their shoulder. At such times, she forgot to hate Maria Krull and even called her 'old girl'.

'You shouldn't drink so much, Pipi! Don't forget you're in mourning.'

'You think I can forget? You think I can forget? If only you knew . . .'

Aunt Maria turned her head towards the door to the kitchen, which had opened, and blinked on seeing Hans in the doorway.

'Do you need something, Hans?'

'No, aunt.'

Pretending not to understand, he sauntered into the shop, like someone planning to stay for a while.

'The thing is, Maria, you landed yourself a good husband, but mine was drunk every night and beat me so much I kept having miscarriages . . . So . . .'

Aunt Maria was embarrassed by the presence of her nephew, who sensed that, without him, she, too, would feel pity and start to lecture Pipi. He sensed more clearly something he had already guessed at: that between the two women there was a complex feeling, a mixture of attraction and hate, a need at times to stand up to one another.

Wasn't it that Aunt Maria saw in Pipi something like a caricature of herself, what she might have become if she hadn't been determinedly virtuous?

And if Pipi kept coming back to the Krulls, sometimes tearful, sometimes insulting, didn't that mean she was unable to do without the grocery?

He opened the door with the Reckitt's sign on it and remained standing there in the doorway, facing the quayside, his back to the two women.

'They're as alike as Joseph and I are alike!' he thought.

It wasn't yet very clear in his mind, but ideas were taking shape, new relationships of cause and effect, subtle links between people.

'What would you have done if your husband had beaten you?' Pipi asked, on her second drink by now.

'I'd have prayed!' Aunt Maria replied, with an impatient glance at Hans, who was still motionless in the doorway.

They couldn't carry on like this, with Hans the way he was! No more than the black cat . . .

It was a story they didn't talk about, because nobody was proud of it. And ever since it had happened, they had refused to have a cat in the house, in spite of the damage caused by mice.

That particular cat was called Beardy. They had got him from a bearded bargee when he was very small, and the name had stuck. He was a very ordinary black cat, a male they had had to neuter because of the smell.

Around the second year, his fur had started to fall out, and they had tried several ointments, without success: Beardy was suffering from a skin disease, and his body was covered in scabs.

'We'll have to drown him,' they would say every day.

And one day Cornelius' assistant was given the task. They gave him an old sack and watched him walk alongside the canal, until well beyond the boatyard.

They didn't talk about it for the rest of the day. Just as they were sitting down to eat, a black cat pushed at the half-open door, rubbed against everyone's legs and sat down in his usual place, in the basket they hadn't thought of removing.

It was Beardy. And from that day on, the cat looked at the people in the house with a strange expression that must have been one of reproach. They all felt so guilty, they didn't dare stroke him any more.

Had a miracle occurred? Within two weeks, his skin disease had healed, but there was still his gaze, his implacable presence, his air of judging everyone . . .

They stood it for a month, two months. They didn't dare try the trick with the sack again. They were ashamed of calling the pound, just for a cat.

It was Joseph, fifteen at the time, who made up his mind to take the animal out in the yard and kill him with a rifle shot at point-blank range.

Hans caused the same kind of unease. He had brought mysterious thoughts into the house, and whenever he looked at the others, it was as if he was judging them in his way.

Aunt Maria was embarrassed to be caught like this, having a friendly conversation with a drunk, a woman who relieved herself in the street and spent at least one night a week at the police station.

Did she guess that Hans was comparing them as if they were interchangeable, as if, for example, circumstances being different, Aunt Maria could have become Pipi and vice versa?

Upstairs, Joseph was gradually finishing his thesis in his fine, regular handwriting. Liesbeth was launching passionately, and happily, into a Chopin étude.

Pipi left. Aunt Maria coughed and finally dared to say:

'Hans!'

He had to be talked to! Too bad!

'Listen, Hans, you shouldn't come into the shop all the time. It's all too easy to see you're a foreigner. We've already had lots of problems, even though we've been in France almost for ever.'

'All right, aunt.'

He smiled, his smile all the more disquieting in that, as he looked at his aunt, he was trying to imagine her peeing at the kerb.

At the same time, he was thinking:

'I bet there are times she envies the old drunk!'

And, aloud:

'In that case, I'll go and spend some time with Anna. That'll help me with my French.'

He knew that Anna would gladly have crossed herself when he approached, as if the devil had appeared. In her case, too, it was because of the temptation!

'You're looking beautiful this morning, Cousin Anna.'

She was hot, because she was making jam and the oven was full on.

'You know I don't like it when you joke.'

Why was it a bad morning for everyone, except for Liesbeth, who still hadn't got over sleeping with Hans?

She was apart from the rest of the family, playing her ringing solo, which penetrated the whole house without arousing an echo in anyone else's heart.

Perhaps it was the threat of a storm, even though there was only one very small white cloud in the sky.

Hans continued teasing Anna, enjoying making her blush, but he did so half-heartedly, without gusto. The truth was, he didn't know what to do with himself. He had too many things on his mind.

And yet nobody could have suspected what was brewing. The ways of chance were far too complicated.

Even when Pipi returned on an errand for the people on a motor barge:

'If you knew the shock it gave me to see him back on the barge! They hadn't warned me . . . He didn't blame me. He's not the kind of man who bears grudges. All he said was . . .'

It was Ninie who started it. She was still going to school. Although the holidays had begun two days earlier, pupils from poorer families who wanted to have a free stay at the seaside had to present themselves at the school with a certificate of poverty to register.

Ninie, who hadn't got over her fear from the previous evening, said to a friend:

'I bet Sidonie was killed by a foreigner.'

'Why a foreigner?'

'Because I know there are some in the area, and yesterday, if me and Germaine had let it happen . . .'

The examining magistrate had so little interest in the case that he had gone on holiday in spite of everything. Admittedly, he owned a small villa just twelve kilometres outside town, and the inspector had been told to phone him if there was any news.

'If you know something, you must tell.'

'Why should I?'

'Because you must!'

'If I'd known that, I wouldn't have said anything.'

The two girls started arguing as they stood in line. The teacher intervened.

'What's going on with the two of you?'

'It's her, miss! She knows who killed Sidonie, but she doesn't want to tell.'

'You know who killed Sidonie?'

'No, miss.'

'Well, then?'

But the other girl insisted:

'She told me that last night a foreigner tried to—'

'That's not true!'

'I swear she told me.'

One thing had led to another. The headmistress, who was

busy with the registrations, had also come to see what was going on. Ninie found herself in the headmistress's office, rigid with embarrassment.

'What did you tell your friend? Don't lie now! If you do, you won't go to the seaside.'

'I told her it must have been a foreigner who did it.'

'Why?'

'Because last night, me and Germaine—'

'Who's Germaine?'

'A friend who runs errands for the shoe shop where Sidonie worked.'

The office still smelled of school.

'Where were you and Germaine?'

'At a dance hall.'

She had dared to admit it, but her courage didn't hold out, and she burst into tears.

Soon afterwards, the headmistress and Ninie walked into the police station of the Saint-Léonard neighbourhood. At two o'clock, a uniformed officer presented himself at the shoe shop and asked for someone called Germaine.

'I haven't done anything!' Germaine protested when they brought her.

The inspector wasn't pleased to have the two girls in his office.

'What did he ask you?'

'If we'd noticed anyone following Sidonie on Sunday night. He must have known her.'

In the guardroom of the station, the officers were in their shirtsleeves, like Joseph Krull in his room.

At four in the afternoon, the sky became overcast, but the same thing had happened in the past few days without the expected storm breaking out. A policeman on a bicycle got off outside the Krull house and went into the shop.

'Do you have anyone foreign here?'

Aunt Maria panicked, immediately thinking of papers not in order and fines.

'We have my husband's nephew who—'

'He's German, isn't he? I'd like to talk to him.'

She walked through the kitchen, which was empty. At the foot of the stairs, she called out:

'Hans! Hans! Someone's asking for you!'

Hans was still teasing Anna as she did the rooms on the first floor.

'I'll be right down, aunt!'

'You're wanted at the station,' the policeman said to him. 'Bring your papers with you. Follow me.'

A few raindrops fell as they turned the corner, making wide circles on the porous cobbles.

Hans saw Germaine and Ninie immediately he entered the inspector's office. They were trying to put on a bold front but didn't dare look him in the face.

'Is this him?'

They nudged each other in mutual encouragement. Germaine stiffened.

'Yes, inspector. And I swear he kept talking about Sidonie . . .'

'Do you have your passport?'

Hans handed it over.

'How come it doesn't have a German visa or a border stamp?'

'Because I sneaked across the border.'

'Why?'

'I was frowned on for my political ideas.'

He was accustomed to police stations and official places in general.

'When I found out they were going to put me in a concentration camp, I took refuge in France.'

'Which way did you come?'

'Via Cologne and Belgium.'

'How did you manage it?'

'When we crossed the border, I hung on to the underside of the carriage.'

This was a Hans the Krulls didn't yet know, a Hans who was terse and sure of himself, defying the authorities.

'Why didn't your relatives declare you as they should have done?'

'I have no idea!'

'Last night, you accosted these girls at the fair. What were your intentions?'

'I didn't have any, inspector!'

'Why did you take them to a dance hall?'

'They asked me to.'

'No!' Germaine cried indignantly.

'Don't forget, I was the first person to notice Sidonie's body in the canal. I even gave you my name. I was there before the bargee.'

'I remember something like that. What of it?'

'Nothing. I was curious, that's all. I told myself that a friend of Sidonie's—'

'How did you know she was her friend?'

'Because I'd seen them together.'

'When?'

Hans paused, and there was an ironic gleam in his eyes. When? If he told them . . .

Well, too bad!

'On Sunday evening.'

'You saw them together on Sunday evening?'

'Yes, inspector, at the fair.'

'Did you already know them?'

Should he also admit that he had previously seen Sidonie under a streetlamp on the quayside, lips glued to a man's?

'No.'

The girls were so overawed that they had moved closer together and were holding hands. As for the inspector, he was furious: all this was horribly complicated, and he foresaw all kinds of pitfalls.

'Why didn't you come to the station earlier?'

'I gave you my name and address. You didn't send for me.'

It was true, damn it! None of this made any sense!

'Be quiet, you two!' the inspector yelled at the girls, because the younger one had whispered a few words in her friend's ear. 'First of all, at your age, you shouldn't be wandering around a fair-ground at night. I'll send you to a reformatory, I will! Especially you, because you're the oldest and you led your companion on.'

He left all three of them in his office and went into the next room to phone the examining magistrate. The girls were so scared that they flattened themselves against the door.

Nobody had wanted this. Sidonie had been dead for a week, and now it was as if Sidonie were coming back to life.

'All right,' the inspector declared at last, bad-humouredly. 'I don't want to arrest you yet. I'll just warn you that you're under surveillance, and I advise you not to leave town. You may go. As for the Krulls . . .'

He didn't say what he would do with the Krulls. He was waiting until he was alone again with the girls and could question them in depth.

'I said you could go.'

Hans shrugged and put his hand on the door knob.

'Goodbye, inspector.'

'Goodbye!'

Hans' last look an involuntary one – was at Germaine's plump figure. The inspector, too, was ogling her big breasts.

5.

Leaving the police station, Hans had the demeanour, the side-long gaze of a street dog on the lookout for trouble.

Rue Saint-Léonard, on which all local business was centred, was a narrow street with trams running down the middle at the level of the pavements. All the houses were shops, mostly food shops that communicated their smells to a whole stretch of the street.

Suddenly Hans' eyes came to rest on a name above a shop front: 'Pierre Schoof'. And below, in thin cursive script: 'Butter, Eggs, Cheese'.

The smell overflowed from its part of the street and mingled with that of the greengrocer's next door, where baskets overran the pavement.

Hans had stopped. He almost stuck his nose to the window, like a dazzled child.

He gazed in at Monsieur Schoof, a Monsieur Schoof who was very different from the way he was when he visited his friends the Krulls, more alert, rounder, with a glowing, fluid cordiality.

In the shop, encased in white marble, three people were serving: Monsieur Schoof, Marguerite in a dazzling white apron and another girl, an assistant who hadn't yet attained the same degree of pinkness as her employers.

The contrast was striking between these three well-groomed people, lacquered like show animals, whose very smiles made you think of something edible, and the resigned, dark-clad housewives, hair pulled back from weary faces, waiting their turn on the other side of the counter and observing the readings on the scales with gloomy anxiety.

Hans went in.

'May I speak to you for a moment, Herr Schoof ?'

He had said this in German, which made Schoof look nervously around. Opening a glass door, he replied in French:

'Come in here. I'll be right with you.'

It was the back room of the shop, a combination dining room, kitchen and lounge, just as shiny as the shop, without a speck of dust, without a mark on the highly polished furniture.

'I'm all yours, Hans . . . It's best not to speak German in the shop. Most people think I'm Dutch, and I prefer it that way . . . What can I offer you?'

In the Krull house, nobody was ever offered a drink, but Monsieur Schoof kept a decanter of cognac and a box of cigars in the dresser.

'I've come to ask your advice, Herr Schoof. I've had some bad news about my father, and I can't bother my Uncle Cornelius.'

Poor Monsieur Schoof, with his round eyes, was already a resigned victim.

'As you may know, my father, who's frowned on by those in power in our country, asked me to cross the border with most of his money. It was the main reason for my journey. Only, I've had to leave the money temporarily in a bank in Belgium, because I was afraid of problems at the French border.'

Monsieur Schoof was listening with one ear, unable to stop himself from also listening to the noises of the shop, the bell at the entrance, the clatter of the till.

'My father has been arrested and taken to a concentration camp. They may shoot him. They may just see to it that he disappears.'

69

'Jesus, Mary and Joseph!' Monsieur Schoof felt obliged to sigh.

'That's why I have to get him out. I've spoken to some specialists, and they're asking me for five thousand francs, which I have to wire this evening to an address we've agreed on. I don't have time to go to Belgium to withdraw the money from the bank. And if I tell my Uncle Cornelius . . .'

Monsieur Schoof hadn't yet moved, didn't seem to have grasped the point of this story.

'I thought that for forty-eight hours you could do me this service . . .'

Monsieur Schoof showed no enthusiasm. He heaved a little sigh, almost looked at his young interlocutor, doubtless told himself it was pointless, that there was no getting out of it, and headed for the till.

From the other end of the counter, Marguerite saw him handling large-denomination notes, understood and threw Hans a curious look.

'I'll be back the day after tomorrow, Herr Schoof . . .'

He was again speaking German in the shop, and to cut short the conversation, Monsieur Schoof dived under the counter.

Hans didn't yet know what he would do with the 5,000 francs. It was an idea that had simply popped into his head as he had stood looking at the shop, and in the same way he now stopped in front of a yellow poster announcing a big concert at the Conservatoire that evening.

He went in and bought two orchestra tickets. When he got back to Quai Saint-Léonard and opened the door of the shop, hearing with the same pleasure as ever the deep-pitched sound of the bell, glancing at the white lion advertising Remy Starch as if saying hello to it, he didn't notice that his Aunt Maria was turning to him anxiously, or that she was following him into the kitchen, or that Anna stopped working and wiped her hands, questioning him with her eyes.

He had almost forgotten about the police station. His aunt was obliged to ask:

'What was it all about?'

'Nothing much. They wanted to know if my papers were in order. Apparently, you're the ones who are in trouble, because you didn't declare that you had a lodger . . . By the way, if Liesbeth wants to go to a concert, I have two tickets . . .'

He realized that they were astonished by the twenty-franc orchestra seats and were sure to ask him where he had got the money. To simplify things, he said:

'I ran into a compatriot of mine. He'd bought the tickets but now he has to leave this evening . . .'

It wasn't over. He had started something that was more complicated than he had thought. Aunt Maria and Anna looked at each other questioningly, worried about letting Liesbeth go out alone with her cousin, but on the other hand uncomfortable at the thought of seeing twenty-franc tickets go to waste.

'What time will it finish?'

He almost replied:

'Whenever you like.'

It didn't matter, since he wouldn't be going to the Conservatoire! Or anywhere else! They didn't need to get into a state about it: he wasn't going to do anything to Liesbeth this evening!

No, all he wanted to do was walk with her and chat. It had suddenly occurred to him that they had never really talked. He had chosen the concert quite by chance, as an excuse, and now it had set the whole household in motion. There was the question of what Liesbeth was going to wear: they would have to iron her blue satin dress and buy new stockings in the neighbourhood!

'Is she going out in a long dress?' he asked.

'To the Conservatoire, always! Especially in the orchestra seats.'

Too bad! That's how it was, and at eight o'clock they were both waiting for the tram at the corner, Liesbeth bare-headed, her hair freshly curled with tongs (she still smelled of burned hair!), a raincoat over her dress, the dress itself skimming the ground.

'Aren't we going to the Conservatoire?' she said in surprise when he got off the tram two stops further on.

'No!'

'Then where are we going?'

'Nowhere!'

He smiled at her cheerfully, as if he had given her a wonderful gift. He even took her hand and walked holding it, like a normal lover.

'I was starting to get bored,' he said.

She misunderstood, obviously, and apologized, humble and timid:

'The house isn't much fun.'

'It's a wonderful house. Don't you like it? As far as I'm concerned, just smelling the wicker . . . Then, when you open the door to the shop . . .'

She wasn't sure if he was joking, but he wasn't.

'And everything in its place. The cups with their brown bottoms hanging from the shelves on the dresser, each with its own little brass hook . . .'

There was always a certain formality in the way he spoke to her. It wasn't out of respect, but rather a sense of distance.

They reached the town centre. The sky had gradually grown lower until it almost touched the roofs of the houses, a cotton-white sky dimmed by the evening and suddenly turning into a fog-like drizzle.

'Let's have a drink. Why don't you sit down there, Liesbeth?'

He had caught sight of the terrace of the Grand Café, with its open plate-glass windows, its motionless waiters, napkins in their hands, and musicians who could be seen on a stage inside, tuning up their instruments and attaching a number to a rail.

'Waiter!'

He just had to cry 'waiter' to be noticed by the whole terrace and for everyone to know that he was German, but he didn't care. On the contrary, it was as if he took pleasure in feeling as foreign as possible.

'Give me a beer and a glass of cognac.'

'Together?'

'Yes, together, and a liqueur for mademoiselle.'

'You want the beer at the same time as the cognac?' the waiter insisted.

Hans took the trouble to explain to Liesbeth:

'That's how we drink where I come from. Don't you do that at home?'

'We never drink spirits or beer.'

After which, he took almost as long to tune up as the orchestra. Finicky, annoyed at not immediately finding the inner and outer mood he was looking for, he sent for cigarettes, refused them and sent the messenger boy back to the tobacconist's, and drank three beers and three glasses of brandy before he felt good.

But then he felt really good, sitting back in his rattan armchair, soaking in the atmosphere.

The drizzle was only visible around the white globes lighting the terrace, and it was more like a luminous dust that was immediately absorbed by the darkness. But the dust was also on the ground, on the black, polished cobbles, except for those under the canopy, which formed a clear rectangle.

The musicians were playing a Viennese waltz with the heavy sentimentality typical of café orchestras. A couple nearby, the man in a bowler hat, the woman with her two hands together on a reticule with a silver clasp, spent a good part of the evening motionless, listening.

Liesbeth didn't dare say a word. She sensed that this was a delicate time, as delicate as the moment they had spent standing silently by the window the previous night.

Never before had the man beside her been so mysterious, so attractive, so formidable.

'I haven't yet told you how my father died,' he said suddenly, as if the story were part of a repertoire. 'It was quite curious! My father was a strange character. You know he was a cobbler, don't you? . . . Have you ever been to Emden?'

'I've never been outside this town.'

'He had a shop beneath the Rathaus. The old palace has arcades, and under these arcades there's a line of shops . . . One fine day, my mother left. We never found out what became of her, and some claim they met her in America . . .'

He was juggling with his characters, his ghosts, mixing them with present realities, the drizzle, the globes of light alive with moths, and even his cousin's tense profile, even her sharp nose, which reminded him of a little girl in Emden in the days when he played in the streets.

'My father at that time was like Cornelius, just as inscrutable, just as severe. He could sit with his leather knife and his awl from six in the morning to eight in the evening, by the window, which was never clean, and not feel any curiosity about what was happening beyond his rectangle of street, beyond the shop on the corner that sold dolls . . . Waiter!'

'Same again?'

'Beer and cognac. The cognac in a larger glass!'

She had never seen him drink before and she was worried, especially when he raised his voice and everyone looked at him. In addition, she was embarrassed by the attention her evening dress was attracting.

'Some say my father won the lottery, but I don't believe that. He never told me about it, because he believed you should never talk about money, that it's the most secret thing there is. What I think happened is that he did well speculating on the mark, which a lot of people did in those days. He bought a shop in Bergenstrasse, with thousands of shoes in cardboard boxes and two girls in black aprons to serve the customers.'

From time to time, a tram stopped abruptly and left again almost immediately.

'Strange, really! Sidonie also worked in a shoe shop.'

Liesbeth shuddered: she hadn't anticipated that they would end up talking about the girl found dead in the canal.

'I met her,' he continued, following the awkward flight of a moth.

'Who, Sidonie?'

'My father's girl. A redhead with a big beauty spot on her chin. He only had eyes for her. Everything revolved around her. He'd spend all day in the shop, hovering over her, and people noticed. I think they were sleeping together . . .'

'Hans!'

'What?'

'Your father!'

'So what? When I say "I think", I mean I'm not sure. He was stupid enough to let himself be led by the nose without getting anything in return! . . . She went out every evening with a clerk from an insurance company who made no bones about picking her up from the shop and looking my father in the eyes as he did so . . . The first time he tried to kill himself, he threw himself in the dock . . .'

'Your father?'

'Yes. They fished him out, although he struggled . . . The girl's name was Eva, I remember. He could have afforded any girl he wanted. I'm sure that apart from my mother he hadn't slept with any other woman. And Eva, on top of everything else, had that redhead smell . . . The fact remains, he did manage to kill himself.

The second time, he made sure. He climbed on to the parapet of the swing bridge with a rope around his neck and a big stone tied to his feet, and before he jumped he shot himself in the head.'

Hans laughed, and she looked at him uneasily, a painful sense of dread in her chest.

'There you are!' he concluded.

And, without transition:

'Has Joseph had lots of girlfriends?'

'I don't know.'

She was lying. He could sense it.

'Answer me,' he insisted spitefully.

'I don't know if he's had lots, but he had one. She was the maid at the Guérins'.'

'The carpenter next door?'

'They didn't really talk about it in front of me. I was only just twelve.'

'So Joseph was nineteen . . . Did he get her pregnant?'

'No!' she protested, turning to make sure that nobody was listening.

'So what happened?'

'Joseph was a sleepwalker. He always has been. When he was little, they put bars on his bedroom window, for fear he'd kill himself. Once, they found him near the lock, and he claimed that a boat had been demanding to be let through for an hour and had stopped him from sleeping . . . Am I boring you, Hans?'

'Go on!'

It was amusing, her fear of displeasing him and at the same time the anxious glances she kept casting around her!

'You know the back of the house. At that time Joseph's room looked out on the yard. One night Mother woke up and saw him walking along the stone ledge that runs across the two houses, the Guérins' and ours. She didn't dare say anything. She thought he was sleepwalking. Then he went into one of the rooms. The next day, she went to see the Guérins, and the maid was dismissed. Joseph was sick for a month and had to be sent to the country . . .'

Hans let out a little laugh that wasn't his usual laugh, perhaps because of everything he had already drunk.

'Do you think I'm like Joseph?' he asked her point-blank, turning his face towards her.

'No! Definitely not!'

'Well, that's where you're wrong. I am like Joseph, or rather, Joseph is like me . . . You wouldn't understand the difference . . . Joseph could have been me and I could have been Joseph. Just as your mother could have been Pipi—'

'Hans!' she ventured to protest against this blasphemy.

'Your mother is so aware of it that she doesn't dare throw Pipi out, even when she insults her. And I bet there are even times when your mother envies her!'

'Pipi?'

'Yes, my dear.'

He laughed again. This was a really good evening! The orchestra was playing some Schubert, and one of the waiters had side whiskers just like in the old days. The streets were so empty by now that you could hear footsteps in the next neighbourhood, make out the route people were taking through the little streets and predict the moment when they would stop and insert their keys in their locks.

'Would you follow me anywhere?'

'Yes.'

'Why?'

She blushed. She didn't dare reply:

'Because I love you!'

But her hand awkwardly searched for his hand, and she squeezed his fingers tight.

'You'd follow me because you're bored at home, isn't that so?'

'That's not the reason, Hans!'

'How did you see the future before you met me?'

'I don't know . . . I'm studying to be a piano teacher.'

'And Joseph to be a doctor!'

'Yes . . . I would probably have stayed in the neighbourhood, but a bit closer to town.'

She felt like crying, for no particular reason. It seemed to her that all of a sudden Hans was trying to diminish her, to diminish her love.

'Why do you ask me that?'

'Who would you have married, for example?'

'I don't know.'

'A shopkeeper? A clerk? . . . Joseph is expected to marry Mademoiselle Schoof, isn't he?'

'I think so.'

'Does he love her?'

'I think so.'

'There you are!' he said smugly, for the second time since they had sat down on the terrace.

As if he had just successfully performed a conjuring trick, or solved a difficult problem on the blackboard!

QED!

'Shall we go home, Hans?'

'Absolutely not!'

'The concert must be over by now.'

'I don't care.'

He took his handkerchief from his pocket and at the same time took out the five 1,000 franc notes and put them down, all crumpled, on the table.

'Hans!'

She was looking at him with that same dread, hardly daring to speak.

'Hans! This money . . .'

'What of it?'

He was more and more cheerful, although his eyes were too shiny.

'True, I could have stolen it!' he said. 'It wouldn't have bothered me. But I didn't. Monsieur Schoof gave it to me.'

'Why?'

'Because I asked him. I wanted money in my pocket. Even if only so that the two of us could leave if things didn't work out.'

'What things?'

'All kinds of things. You never know.'

'He gave you all that money, just like that?'

'Just like that, yes! I told him a story. It would take too long to explain . . . Waiter!'

He paid with a large-denomination note, then changed his mind and asked for another glass of cognac, heedless of his cousin's reproachful look.

'That's how I see life!' he declared, getting to his feet.

He knocked over a chair as they left the terrace, then turned to look at the café all lit up, two elderly men playing backgammon in a corner, the woman at the till starting to cash up.

'It's late, Hans. I bet it's nearly midnight.'

She reached for his arm, took little steps to keep up with him, didn't quite know what to say, or how to deal with him.

He was the cock of the walk and she was merely a little chicken who wasn't yet used to it, as terrified as she was attracted.

'Where are we going?' she asked anxiously, as he turned into a dark street.

'We're walking home via the quayside.'

'It's late, Hans!'

He really didn't care. He lit a cigarette and said:

'I don't know anything more arousing than the sight of a couple in some dark corner at night. You don't know quite what they're doing. You can imagine all kinds of things. You can almost smell their saliva, and something else . . .'

'Hans!'

'When Joseph sees that, his fingers start shaking.'

'Have you seen him do that?'

'Oh, yes! He'd like to be in the man's shoes, in the shoes of all men who make love. He'd like to undress every woman, caress her . . .'

'Aren't you exaggerating, Hans?'

'I don't think so . . . There, look!'

He stopped her not far from a house where they could see a lighted window on the first floor, a blind made golden by the light inside, the silhouette of a woman. She wasn't so easy to make out, but you could certainly imagine that she was undressing. Just then, another silhouette, the head of a man, emerged from the depths of the room, where the bed must have been.

'I'm sure that if Joseph were here . . .'

'What would he do?'

'Nothing. He'd break out in a cold sweat. He'd swallow. His hands would shake, and he'd look in every dark corner, like a dog sniffing dustbins, in the mad hope of coming across a woman delayed on her way home . . .'

She shivered, and he felt it.

'What's the matter?'

'You're scaring me.'

'Hasn't Joseph ever scared you?'

'Not until now. But now I'm not going to be able to look at him . . . Is it true, Hans, that you'll never leave here without me?'

'I think so,' he said pensively.

'Aren't you sure?'

He stopped her under a streetlamp. He looked at her, face slightly wet from the drizzle, which was easing off.

Her eyes were anxious, her features drawn, but there was happiness all the same on her thin face with its sharp nose.

'Come . . .'

Her dress was going to be soiled at the bottom, being too long for the muddy streets and especially for the quayside.

They could see the lock in the distance, black on grey, barges with rough white stripes painted on them, empty benches between the trees.

He repeated:

'Come . . .'

'What do you want to do, Hans?'

Then, a moment later:

'Not here . . .'

'Shh!'

She was looking around her with terror. It seemed to her that people were going to emerge from the shadows, that eyes were watching her from behind every tree. And, on top of everything else, something in her underwear was starting to tear.

'If Joseph could only see us!' he sneered.

She didn't cry. She was too scared. But it was the most horrible minute of her life. She felt nothing. She was listening, listening so hard she could hear every drop of water on the foliage of the trees, a dog pulling on a chain in a yard.

'Hans . . .'

He let go of her, looked at her with a smile.

'What?'

'I don't understand . . . You . . . Watch out!'

They had distinctly heard footsteps. They saw shadowy figures, three of them, coming along the street. The one in the middle was a woman. The other two were recognizable as police officers, because of their caps, and they each held one of the woman's arms, giving her a shake from time to time.

'You're brutes! Brutes!' she was saying.

'Pipi . . .' Liesbeth murmured.

'So what?'

'I don't know . . . I'm scared . . .'

'Scared of what?'

'Of everything . . .'

Perhaps even of the barges, which looked like big beasts crouching in the water, or of the posts of the swing bridge . . .

Hadn't Hans mentioned a swing bridge from which his father . . .

'Let's go straight home!'

Moreover, she always felt physically sick when he'd just had his way with her, and it seemed to her that her whole being bore visible traces.

The two policemen and the woman had turned into the first street, which led to the police station. Liesbeth stumbled as she walked.

'We shouldn't have done it,' she said mechanically.

Then she seized hold of his arm again, came to a halt and pointed to a thin thread of light beneath a ground-floor door in the row of unlighted houses.

'They haven't gone to bed yet!'

'What difference does that make?'

'There's a light on in the shop!'

'So what?'

'They never put the light on in the shop at night. Something's happened. I have a bad feeling about this . . .'

He shrugged and drew her after him, lighting another cigarette while she inserted the key in the lock. But the door swung open. Aunt Maria was there, very upright, as pale and grey as her hair.

'There you are,' she said in a neutral voice.

Anna was sitting on the stool that was used to reach the upper shelves, and for the first time Hans saw her crying, her eyes big and red, her distorted face making her look ten years older.

Joseph was looking at his cousin with dry eyes, but with an impressive fixity.

As for Liesbeth, she took a few steps forwards and threw an

anxious look all around. Receiving no answer to her silent interrogation, she said in an imploring voice:

'What's the matter? What's going on?'

'Shh!'

Her mother pointed at the ceiling. That meant that her father was asleep and had to be kept out of all this.

'Mother!' Liesbeth begged.

Turning her head away, Aunt Maria said:

'That woman came . . .'

'Pipi?'

A nod.

'She knocked at the door and yelled insults.'

Aunt Maria's eyes came to rest for a moment on Hans, who was standing with his back up against the counter, looking at the transparent sign for Remy Starch: the blue looked much darker than during the day, because of the shutter behind it.

'She's saying now that . . .'

Maria Krull was finding it difficult to speak. Her lower lip was quivering, and her features had clouded over, making her look more like Anna, who suddenly burst into tears again.

'She's saying we're the ones who . . .'

She couldn't stand it any more. The look of pain spread until it convulsed her whole face, and she hid behind her cottonette apron with its small check pattern, which was always so carefully starched.

'Mother!'

Liesbeth rushed towards her, but her mother shrugged as if to say:

'Leave me alone! . . . I can't stand it any more . . .'

While Joseph, motionless in his corner, looked down harshly at the grey floor.

6.

Suddenly they all froze, and there was silence. Each remained as he or she was, Aunt Maria with her face half hidden by her apron, Liesbeth anxious and imploring, Joseph with his head bowed and, behind the counter, Anna crying, ridiculous in petticoat and camisole, her hair pinned up.

The last noise had been a sniffle from Aunt Maria, and now there was a void. Hans opened his mouth to speak, then changed his mind in time on discovering, near the glass door of the kitchen, what it was that had immobilized them: Cornelius. They hadn't heard him coming, but there he was, looking at them. Not asking any questions, just looking.

He wasn't inquisitive, or suspicious, or ironic, or anything else. He was simply there.

And the others didn't know how to extricate themselves from the gestures that had been frozen when they had realized that he was there. Aunt Maria was embarrassed by her own tears. Liesbeth would have liked to smile. They didn't even know exactly how long he had been there, in some corner of the dark house!

'It must have been children . . . or a drunk,' Anna suddenly had the presence of mind to say. 'Don't cry, mother.'

Cornelius was trying to understand, frowning just a little.

'Somebody threw a stone at the shutter and broke a windowpane.'

Cornelius slowly looked round until his eyes came to rest on the shop window. The shutter was closed but, against that shutter, the uneven fragments of glass were clearly visible, and there was a distinct draught.

'We'll have to call the glazier,' Cornelius said. 'Shall we go to bed?'

That was all he said. They all followed him up the stairs, without another word. Aunt Maria was the last up, remaining behind to switch off the lights, and they heard her sniffle one last time. In the corridor on the second floor, Liesbeth's hand brushed Hans'.

In each cell of the house, sleep was long in coming. Drizzle was still falling over the town.

Hans slept late, as was his habit when he had been drinking. He was naked on his bed. The window was open, and the sun was bright on the big trees, with a purer light than the previous days. The air was better, too, with a keener taste.

Eyes closed, limbs stretched, Hans savoured the little waves of air that came in through the window, swelled the curtain in passing and at last slid over his skin.

All the sounds merged together: the din of the lock, the bell of the tram, the noises from downstairs and the hammers of the boat-builder's. His thoughts merged too. He didn't so much think them as dream them, and they coalesced around Anna, but an Anna whose face looked strange, almost poetic, in a way that intrigued and attracted him.

Then, without transition, because of a fly that came to rest on his lip, he was up, a sly look in his eye, a bad taste in his mouth. For a long time, he scratched his scalp, while his eyes gradually accustomed themselves to the light and made out the trees, the water of the canal, the stern of a brown barge adorned with brass lettering.

As he took two steps forwards, something grabbed his attention, and the last wisps of sleep faded. His eyes more focused now, he looked down and beyond the central reservation, where two dogs were chasing each other, to the beginning of the lock, where a group of people stood, Pipi in the middle. They were looking towards the Krull house, and Pipi was gesticulating.

All alone in his room, Hans clicked his tongue, which must have meant:

'Oh, well!'

Followed by a shrug. It wasn't his fault! He brushed his teeth and dressed, glancing every now and again at the lock, where a boat was rising and the bargees still surrounded Pipi.

Nothing had happened yet, but all the same, Hans, who wasn't impressionable, felt the need to look at himself in the mirror and keep repeating that it wasn't his fault.

He heard Liesbeth walk into her room next door. That meant it was about ten, and she was going to make her bed, empty her waste water and do some dusting, while Anna, as soon as her lunch was on the stove, would come and perform the same chores in Hans' room.

Hans went out and, seeing Liesbeth's door open, took a couple of steps, without any kind of intention, simply to say good morning to her, perhaps to ask her if her mother had got over the previous night's upset.

Liesbeth was bent forwards, turning over the mattress on her bed. She gave a start, turned and, against all expectation, put a finger to her lips and gestured to him to go.

Once again, Hans shrugged. Why did he go downstairs noiselessly, without making a single step creak? It wasn't premeditated. He reached the ground-floor corridor, where it was always cooler than elsewhere and where the floor was covered in large blue tiles. Hearing voices, he recognized his aunt's.

He didn't need to see. Anna was sitting in front of the table with its red check oilcloth, peeling vegetables, while Aunt Maria, as always, was standing near the glass door leading into the shop, from which sunlight filtered through the guipure curtain.

'. . . didn't want to say!'

It was the end of a sentence. She was sighing. The characteristic scraping of the knife on the vegetables, doubtless carrots, could be heard.

'. . . When people saw one more foreigner in our house . . .'

Aunt Maria's head must be bowed, Anna assuming a sad, dignified air.

'. . . Especially as he hasn't done anything to pass unnoticed! On the contrary! . . . When I think how hard it was for us at the beginning. And even later! During the war . . . you were too small . . . your father was mobilized in a railway station on the outskirts of Paris . . . One day, a drunk I refused to serve a drink got it into his head, on the way out, to use the word "spy". I thought they were going to break everything, smash the shop window, throw the furniture out into the street, just like they did to the Lipmanns, although the Lipmanns weren't naturalized . . .'

Heard through the door, it was like a deep, regular hum. Hans did not move.

'When the fire broke out at the Rideau yard, there were people who said it was us, because of our name . . .'

And, in another tone:

'I'm glad the glazier's coming.'

She put more coal on the fire, mechanically, thinking of something else.

'Has Liesbeth said anything to you?'

'No, Mother. About what?'

'Nothing . . . She's the one who's most often with him.'

'Because he runs after her!' Anna asserted. 'The sooner he goes, the better it'll be for every—'

Just as she was about to say '—body', he opened the door and repeated:

'Everybody! . . . Good morning, aunt! Good morning, Anna! Have you kept a little coffee for me?'

He took down a cup and poured himself coffee from the pot standing on a corner of the stove.

'So Pipi's back, is she?' he said.

'She's out there, by the lock.'

'So I saw!'

Oh, yes, he had seen! He should have realized that he was in the way, but he didn't say anything about leaving. He was smiling! He was cheerful! He was enjoying the sun, the quality of the air, the smell of the shop and the sight of the vegetables spread out on the table!

Couldn't he see that the windowpane being broken in that sinister way was like the first wound to the house? Every time Aunt Maria turned in that direction – which she did constantly – she felt so disturbed that she would pass her hand over her eyes.

'Where are you going, Hans?'

He had drunk his coffee and was heading towards the quayside.

'To listen to what she's saying!'

'Hans, please don't do that, I beg you! It's the best way to get her even more worked up!'

'All right. I won't go.'

They were to remember that morning, when there was still nothing but a broken pane of glass, when the air was limpid, when you could see families passing by, off on their holidays.

Nobody was thinking about Sidonie. Even Pipi had probably forgotten, at least partly, that all this was about her, that the start of everything had been another sunny morning when a naked white form had been pulled out of the water.

Today, it was all about the Krulls, and people were looking at their house from a distance, the brown-painted shop, the name in slanted letters: 'C. Krull'.

From time to time, their neighbour, the carpenter's wife, appeared in her doorway to make sure that nothing was happening, that there was still nothing but a broken pane of glass.

Nothing happened until midday, except that they saw Potut pass by and take a seat on the bench where he sometimes dozed for hours on end.

On the other hand, no customers came in, and the shop bell remained silent. Out there at the lock and in the harbour, Pipi was turning them away. If they had errands for her to run, she went all the way to Rue Saint-Léonard.

The glazier came at 11.30 and set to work. The son of the Rideaus, a little boy, watched him for a while, until the carpenter's wife called out:

'You really should go home, Émile! Don't stay outside that house!'

Aunt Maria heard. Hans, who was in the kitchen, turned to her, and their eyes met.

He wasn't laughing now. There was a new solemnity in his eyes.

'What did Joseph say?' he asked.

Maria Krull hadn't expected that. She couldn't help shuddering and raising her head to the ceiling.

'He's busy with his thesis.'

So busy that, when he came down, he had the staring eyes of someone who has overslept. He gave a start as soon as anybody spoke to him.

They ate, each in his or her usual place. From his, Hans could see outside through the half-open door. Aunt Maria was on the same side as him, which was how they both discovered the new group, while a stew that nobody was enjoying steamed on the table.

Germaine, the plump, short-legged girl now famous in the Saint-Léonard neighbourhood, was sporting the most ridiculous hat, one most calculated to add a touch of the grotesque to her figure: a rimless cherry-red straw cloche, which made her look like a gnome.

What made the resemblance even stronger was her seriousness, her air of self-importance, the way she nodded when she had just said something, as if insisting:

'That's right! That's the way it is.'

And her big eyes, like a doll that hadn't quite come out right . . .

There she was, just opposite the house, on the other side of the street, accompanied by two girls and a young man who all worked in the same shoe shop. She was making no attempt to pass unnoticed, or to pretend to be busy with something else. On the contrary! She was gesticulating, pointing at the house, then at one of the upstairs windows, nobody was quite sure why.

Because from the kitchen, they couldn't hear what she was saying. They could only see. And even then, only Aunt Maria and Hans! They heard their neighbour's door open and close. The carpenter's wife, obviously, coming to watch the show.

Unable to resist her curiosity for very long, she crossed the road and questioned Germaine, who solemnly resumed her explanation with a profusion of gestures.

Going to get a pot from the fire, Liesbeth saw the scene and turned anxious eyes, not to her family, but to Hans.

'Has he replaced the glass?' asked Cornelius, who had his back to the street.

'Yes. He just finished.'

'How much did he charge?'

'Anna, how much did he charge? You paid him.'

'I didn't pay, because he didn't have the bill. He has to ask his boss.'

Ordinary words, everyday gestures. The stew, followed by the plum compote.

On the quayside, Potut had left his bench and was now standing near Germaine, who was still talking. She was capable of talking for ever, with the same exaggerated solemnity, like a child taking herself seriously, the same categorical gestures, the same defiant glances at the Krull house.

Wasn't she at least going to go home to eat?

Cornelius lit his pipe, as serene as a saint in his niche. Joseph's right hand tensed. He stood up and went and planted his tall frame in the doorway. All they could see was his back.

'Serve the coffee, Liesbeth.'

She dropped a cup, which broke the spell, at least long enough for her mother to be able to say:

'What are you doing? You're all fingers and thumbs these days!'

Joseph turned. His Adam's apple was going up and down. He headed for the other door, the one that led to the corridor and the stairs.

'Aren't you having your coffee?'

He hesitated, then decided he wouldn't.

'I'm going upstairs.'

'You should rest a little.'

She didn't really think that. She knew it wasn't possible. But she had to pretend, at least for Cornelius.

The most worrying thing was that, after finishing his coffee, it was the old man's custom to stand in the doorway of the shop for a while, smoking his pipe.

Today was no different. Germaine was still opposite, with

her horrible red hat. Just then, a little slip of a girl was starting to write something in chalk on the wall of the house. She had only written the first letter. The arrival of Cornelius made her run away with a cry of terror. Making a detour, she joined the others on the central reservation.

Against all expectation, it was Hans who from time to time sought Aunt Maria's eyes, it was with Hans that she was having something like a silent conversation.

'This is serious, isn't it?' she seemed to be saying.

He was making no attempt to persuade her of the contrary. If she could, she would already have asked him:

'What are we going to do?'

Even though there was still nothing, just a broken window-pane that had immediately been replaced, a drunk woman rousing the bargees near the lock and a little girl with a woman's calves and buttocks standing outside the house, enjoying the spectacle of her new-found importance!

When Cornelius came back inside, they were worried about what he was going to say, how he would react. But there was no reaction at all. He still had his ivory complexion, his grey eyes under grey eyebrows, his stiff beard, and his slippers slid over the floor as he crossed the kitchen, just like any other day, put his pipe back on the rack and headed for the workshop.

It was Liesbeth who yielded first and cried out:

'She's not going away!'

'Calm down,' her mother murmured. 'Don't keep showing yourself.'

And for a while she remained motionless, her eyes half closed, her lips alone moving regularly: her hands joined across her belly, she was praying over the uncleared table, over her plate on which there were seven plum stones.

Then a piercing voice echoed in the crystalline air, a shrill, vulgar working-class woman's voice:

'Germaine! . . . Germaine!'

The second syllable was dragged out. The monster in the red hat replied, just as shrilly:

'Coming, Mum!'

And the group in front of the house melted away. The only person remaining was Potut, with his bad feet, who headed straight for the nearest bench. The area was clear but for the trees and the stones, on which the sun played.

Maria Krull sighed and looked at Hans in relief.

She had said, seeing him grab his jacket:

'I don't think you should go out, Hans!'

He had only reflected for a moment and had decided to stay.

They were trying hard to act as they did on other days. Liesbeth was playing the piano in the lounge, although her mother had wondered if it was right, on such a day, for music to issue forth from the house like that.

'People will get tired of it in the end!' Hans had asserted, as if reading her mind.

From one hour to the next, the subtle bond between him and his aunt was growing stronger. It was as if they alone understood, they alone knew or guessed certain things, they alone, of everyone in the house, were grown-ups.

'What are you doing, Anna?' Maria said in surprise, seeing Anna come back with a handkerchief knotted around her hair and a bucket of water in each hand.

'It's the day for the shop, Mother.'

Another hesitation. Should they go ahead with the usual weekly cleaning of the shop?

They did so. The street door remained open while the scrubbing brush went back and forth on the tiled floor and rivulets of soapy water zigzagged across the doorstep.

Aunt Maria worked with her daughter. Sometimes on the

stool, sometimes not, she would pick up all the jars, all the boxes, all the packets of merchandise, shelf by shelf, wipe the woodwork, and every now and again go outside to shake her dust cloth.

Most of the time, Hans watched them, standing between the kitchen and the shop, smoking his cigarette, but sometimes he went to the workshop, an oasis of peace, half-light and coolness. There, nothing was different from any other day, or from how it had been twenty or thirty years earlier. The bundles of wicker, some of white wicker, others of unpeeled wicker, stood against the whitewashed walls. Old Cornelius sat in his corner, on a chair whose legs had been half sawn off, and the assistant occupied a similar chair two metres from him, making a similar basket, at the same speed, neither of them ever thinking of talking.

In all the years, almost a lifetime, that this had been going on, the blue rep cushion on Cornelius' chair had never been changed!

The door was open, revealing grass between the cobblestones in the yard, and a little free space, an area of black earth, around the lime tree. Birds were singing, and a blackbird hopped in the bright rectangle that constituted the two men's horizon.

The assistant was a hunchback. He always arrived at six in the morning and left, by the back door, just before nightfall. It was hard to imagine the world in which he spent his time until the next day.

More piano chords! Liesbeth kept on stubbornly, stumbling in the same place and resuming nervously, then racing ahead and stumbling again in an identical manner.

'Hans!'

Aunt Maria, who had called him, merely said to him in a low voice:

'Go and have a look outside.'

The pavement was deserted, baking in the sun. He looked right and left and only then at the shop front, where, beneath the window, on the dark brick, big, clumsy downstrokes formed the word 'Murderers'.

Pipi was nowhere to be seen. The lock was empty. The world seemed asleep and yet, while the two women were in the grocery, the door constantly open, someone had approached, perhaps the little girl from earlier, and written that word.

It was just a word. Sidonie might not have been as dead as she had been but she wasn't yet being mentioned on the quayside on the edge of town.

It was still abstract.

Murderers, *in the plural!*

And above the window, the word 'Krull'.

'I should wipe it off, shouldn't I, Hans?'

Even Anna now was stopping in front of him, a wet cloth in her hand, and asking him for advice!

The letters couldn't be entirely wiped off. Chalk remained in the pores of the brick, and from a distance the word could be reconstructed.

'Go back in, Hans. Don't stay there.'

The reason he had lingered for a moment out on the street was to look up at Joseph, still in his shirtsleeves by his window, bent over his exercise books.

All this was as fragile as the air, as the landscape a few moments, a few fractions of a second, before a powder keg explodes.

They were performing the same actions as any other day, but these actions seemed more muffled than usual. When they spoke, they imagined they were speaking naturally, but the voices didn't have their familiar sound. They washed the floor. Aunt Maria polished the brass pans of the scales, then the zinc part of the counter, where drinks were served.

And all the while they were thinking of their enemies! They didn't know where they were, or what they were planning.

At five, suddenly, even though the shoe shop didn't close until 6.30, there was the red hat, and Germaine, this time with other girls, half a dozen street girls like her, whom she must have gathered from the dead-end street where she lived.

They were laughing and raising their voices. Germaine was no longer as overawed as she had been at midday. She had the idea of sending one of her friends into the shop, just to see. Before that, they clubbed together to amass a few sous.

The one who came in was a black-haired beanpole, feet bare in old shoes, legs grey with dust.

'Chocolate!' she said bad-temperedly, approaching the counter.

'What kind?'

'The twenty-sou kind.'

She was looking Aunt Maria in the eyes, muscles tense, clearly ready to run away at the first unsettling gesture.

Aunt Maria put her hand in a jar and fished out a piece of chocolate wrapped in purple paper. The girl pushed her twenty sous across the counter. Was she planning something else, an act of heroism, insulting Maria for example, or throwing the chocolate on the floor? You could see the temptation on her face, but she didn't dare. She grabbed the purple paper, took two steps normally and finally ran off to join her companions.

One of them, spotting Maria Krull's forehead and eyes above the window display, stuck her tongue out. But Germaine scorned such childishness. Her role was far too important for that. She was content to stand there and look defiantly in the direction of the shop.

What mysterious association of ideas led Aunt Maria, a few moments later, to ask Hans, who had just poured himself a glass of lemonade:

'Hasn't your father written to you, Hans?'

He sensed the suspicion in her voice. They were almost as cunning as each other.

'It would put him in a compromising position.'

'Oh?'

'I'm out of favour politically.'

She didn't insist, announced:

'I'm going to have a wash.'

The still damp shop smelled clean. Anna, her apron soaked, her hair dishevelled, shook herself and murmured:

'So am I.'

But it only took a look from her mother for her to realize that it was unwise to leave Hans alone in the shop, and she changed her mind.

'No, when you come back down! What if someone comes in?'

The words reverberated. They had been involuntary, which made them all the more striking. Since the morning, nobody had come in apart from the girl, who could be seen licking her piece of chocolate on the quayside.

The quayside itself seemed emptier than usual, and in that emptiness all that was left was that stubborn red hat, that disgusting Germaine who, an hour later, was joined by Ninie, tall, her face askew.

What had Ninie been doing all day? Why hadn't she, too, come to the quayside? And what about Pipi? Or Potut, who had been asleep on a bench earlier and had now disappeared?

The workers from the Rideau boatyard passed at six, as they always did, but this time they stopped. One of them called out to Germaine, who launched into a long speech.

They were in their work clothes. They were looking at the name 'Krull'. They were becoming bad-tempered.

In the end, though, they left without doing anything. After which, it was the turn of a policeman on a bicycle to stop at the kerb. He didn't even bother to get off. As the shop door was open, to let the tiles dry, he merely called out:

'Anyone there?'

Anna went out and he handed her a paper.

'What is it?' Hans asked when she came back inside.

'A summons for Father. He has to present himself at the police station tomorrow at nine o'clock. I think Mother will go instead.'

And indeed, they didn't show the summons to Cornelius or even tell him about it. They respected him. He was the head of the family. But, perhaps for the very reason that they feared and respected him, he was kept out of most things that happened.

It was striking, all the more so in that he had the calm, the dignity of a deaf person pursuing his inner dreams while everyone about him gets excited.

Whenever he entered the kitchen, everyone fell silent, and he seemed to find this silence natural. They were silent as they ate, apart from a few banal or necessary phrases. They were silent until he left, and the silence accompanied him into the workshop, where he rejoined his assistant.

'Where's Liesbeth?' Aunt Maria asked, slipping the summons inside her blouse.

The piano having fallen silent, they had no idea where Liesbeth was. They called her name up the stairs.

Hans had disappeared, too.

In reality, they had just met up in the corridor on the second floor. Hans had gone up to get cigarettes. Liesbeth had been waiting for him.

She clung to him with an imploring air.

'I can't stand it any more!'

Was that his fault? Passionately, she continued:

'Let's leave here!'

Her mother's voice called:

'Liesbeth!'

'I'll be right down!'

However hard she tried to hypnotize Hans, he didn't give her the gesture of approval she had been expecting.

'I'm coming!'

She rearranged her hair, mechanically, still turning to him . . .

'What were you doing up there?'

'Nothing! Washing my hands.'

'Were you with Hans?'

'No. Why? Isn't he here?'

Hans was leaning over the banisters, listening and clicking his tongue like a connoisseur.

Was it that Aunt Maria didn't get to sleep that night? Or was she woken by an unusual noise? Hans became aware in his sleep of whispering outside in the street. Had his aunt heard it, too, and woken completely?

He himself woke up because someone touched his shoulder. It was Liesbeth, in her nightdress, signalling to him to be quiet. Dawn had broken, although it was still indistinct, more grey than pink.

'Go and have a look downstairs,' she whispered.

And, as if to better explain what she wanted, she went to the window and cautiously leaned out.

He stood up and put on his pyjamas, which he never wore in bed.

'What is it?'

She made it clear to him that she didn't know. He tiptoed downstairs and through the kitchen. The door to the shop was open, and he went in.

Aunt Maria was there, crouching, a cloth in her hand. She looked up in fright, and when she saw it was Hans she put a finger to her mouth.

It was only four in the morning. There wasn't a soul on the quayside, apart from Aunt Maria, who was cleaning the doorstep.

This was probably the first time in her life that she had shown herself outside in other than her day clothes.

'What's going on?' he asked her with his eyes.

The smell told him. Then the sight, when he was quite close to it. During the night, someone had covered the doorstep with excrement, which his aunt was busy removing.

Hans' shoulder brushed against something soft. He looked up and saw a dead cat, also smeared in excrement, hanging from the bell.

Aunt Maria carried out her task without disgust, afraid only that she might not have tidied everything up by the time Cornelius came down at 5.30, as he always did.

When she saw Hans take down the cat, she gave him a look of gratitude.

Then, still with gestures, fearing that the slightest noise might wake the house, she pointed to the brown shutter.

On it, in letters more than a metre high, a word had been written, in oil paint this time: 'Kill'.

7.

Just after 8.30, Maria Krull, who had gone up to her room, came back down, ready to go out, but in her everyday clothes, her woollen dress, her black hat, her linen gloves and her shoes with their turned heels.

There was a mirror in the bamboo coatstand at the foot of the stairs, and, as she always did, she looked in it to adjust her hat.

This time, it was herself and not the hat that she seemed to be looking at. She was quite grey this morning, ash grey, not just her hair, but her complexion, her voice, her movements.

There was a surprised contact between the living eyes and the eyes in the mirror, then Aunt Maria, instead of walking through the kitchen and the shop to go out, went back up to the first floor.

Anna was washing the breakfast dishes, occasionally looking out at the quayside beyond the shop. Liesbeth, because her mother had told her to, had sat down at her piano and was turning the pages of a score while listening to the noises of the house. Hans must have been in the workshop or the yard.

Maria Krull was moving about in her room, and when she came back down again, a few moments later, she had put on the black silk dress she used for special occasions, with the jade jewellery, the gold chain with the clasp, the half-veil and the white gloves.

She didn't need to look at herself again in the mirror. She was in a hurry. She set off as if nothing was going to stop her but retraced her steps, leaned towards Anna and kissed her on the cheek, without a word, then went into the lounge and kissed Liesbeth twice.

When she came back along the corridor, Hans was there, and she gave a start, hesitated, left at last without having said a word. Or rather, she had murmured to Anna, in her most normal voice:

'If your father asks for me, say I've gone to the market.'

Hans went to the doorway to watch her go. She was hurrying, in spite of herself, looking down at her feet, and Hans could have sworn her lips were moving, that as she walked she was rehearsing in a low voice the words she would say to the inspector . . .

Was it only an impression caused by Aunt Maria's absence? There were strange gaps in the house that morning, what aviators call air pockets. You walked across a room and felt uncomfortable because it didn't have its usual density, because it didn't smell the same, because you didn't hear a noise you should have heard. Liesbeth was in the lounge, for instance, sitting at her piano, but even though it was time for her practice, no note emerged from the instrument.

Outside, too, the landscape was emptier today. Were there really fewer boats in the harbour? It was possible, because it was the start of the off-season. There was some washing out to dry, but not much of it, and in the overly still air it hung motionless.

Pipi wasn't at the lock. She had probably drunk too much the day before and was sleeping it off.

Once the shutter had been raised, the Krull grocery bore no trace of the night's abuse, and the door was left open as if to assert that nothing had changed and they had no reason to hide.

At a loose end, Hans came back into the kitchen and, as was his habit, lifted the lids of the saucepans, which was calculated to get Anna in a rage.

She said nothing. Perhaps she didn't notice. Everything was muffled, everything was subdued, and the sounds from outside came from further away than usual.

'What are we doing for lunch?' he asked.

'I have no idea.'

It wasn't in order not to answer him. She really had no idea. Hans continued on his way, walked down the always cool corridor and opened the door to the lounge.

He found the piano closed, Liesbeth with both elbows on the lid, her chin on her hands, staring at a score she didn't see. He passed behind her and gently stroked the short blonde hair on the back of her neck.

First, she moved her head to let him know she wanted to be left alone. He persisted, smiling, and she sighed:

'Leave me be, Hans!'

He kept on stroking her, still smiling, sliding his hand down her back, under her dress and into the hollow between her shoulder blades.

Then, with an instinctive movement, she turned, genuine anger on her face, and cried:

'Please leave me alone!'

Her anger had no sooner burst out than she regretted it, looked at Hans anxiously, then turned her head away, murmuring:

'I'm sorry . . . I'm on edge . . .'

He stopped teasing her. Adapting to the tempo of the house, he went and took a chair, sat down astride it next to Liesbeth, in silence, and lit a cigarette. The window, with its net curtain and two green plants in copper pots on either side, was closed, as was the door, and they were alone, surrounded by flowered wallpaper, family photographs, polished furniture and trinkets.

It was as if Hans knew that Liesbeth was going to speak, wanted to speak. He was waiting, in the pose of someone listening, and she said, as if to get started:

'Don't look at me like that.'

Then, in a lower voice, turning towards the piano:

'Sometimes I feel ashamed of myself . . .'

But he wasn't ashamed, either of himself or of her. He didn't even feel sorry for her. But he was savouring the show, the moment, from the atmosphere of the lounge to the line of Liesbeth's neck, her sharp nose, the little handkerchief rolled into a ball in her hand in preparation for any eventuality.

'Mother has suffered so much! She's struggled all her life! And all I've done was . . .'

What he said in reply to this was not at all what she expected. Calmly, blowing cigarette smoke, he asked:

'Why has she suffered?'

It was the only difficult moment to get through, the hurdle to be cleared. Either she was going to cry, run out and take refuge in her room, or she would talk like a reasonable person. And that was what happened, not all at once, and still with hesitations, with moments of shyness and awkwardness, but with a growing calm.

'People have been so awful to us!'

'Why?'

'Because of everything! Because we're foreigners! At school, the children called me the Kraut, and the teacher would say to me in front of the whole class: "Mademoiselle, when one receives a country's hospitality, one has double the duty to behave well."'

The door opened, and Anna looked in. Her face as grey as her mother's, she looked at the couple sitting there calmly and merely sighed:

'So this is where you are, is it?'

She went out as she had come. The door closed behind her noiselessly. Liesbeth took the opportunity to say:

'Anna was even less lucky. She was almost engaged to a very respectable young man, the son of the justice of the peace who owns the house with the two balconies opposite the church of Saint-Léonard. When his father found out, he sent his son away to continue his studies in Montpellier and swore that he would disown him if he married my sister . . . What can we do? Mother never hits back. She's friendly to everyone. But I know it upsets her when neighbours, people like the Morins, who live just next door, prefer to put their hats on and go shopping somewhere else.'

Her voice grew even lower, in preparation for a more solemn admission.

'Mother is so deserving, Hans! If only you knew . . .'

She was going to tell him, of course, but she owed it to herself to hesitate, to look around to make sure that nobody was listening.

'When father arrived here, going from town to town as artisans did in those days, the firing range didn't exist yet and the parade ground was a vast osier bed. The Rideau boatyard wasn't here either: I think it was the municipal dump. Father, who didn't speak French, settled in a wooden shack on the other side of the water, surrounded by osiers, and started making baskets. We used to have a photograph of him at that time, but it faded. He was already like he is now, except that his beard was fair, although in the photograph it looked white . . .'

She broke off, pricked up her ears. There was someone in the shop. The two of them listened for a moment, expecting a scene, and were reassured when they recognized the sound of coins in the till, followed by footsteps on the pavement.

It had been a customer!

*

'Where the carpenter lives now, there was a little farm where the townspeople came to drink milk on Sundays.'

'And this house?'

'It was only one storey in those days, and where the yard is now was part of the farm's dung heap. The harbour already existed. Mother says there were more boats than today, all horse-drawn. This was where the bargees came to drink. We didn't yet have the grocery, but only drinks for the men and oats for the horses.'

She was at last talking like a reasonable person, and in the oasis of the lounge with its flowered wallpaper, the anguish of the house had melted away. The smoke from Hans' cigarette wrapped itself around the ceiling light. Sparrows hopped on the window ledge.

'We never talk about these things. Anna knows more about it than I do, because she's older. She knew our grandmother.'

'Aunt Maria's mother?'

'Yes. She was the one who ran the bar.'

'All by herself?'

'At first, yes. I never found out where exactly she came from, but she was a southern type. Apparently she was a beautiful woman . . . Mother was very good-looking, too.'

'And her father?'

'That's precisely why I said that Mother's so deserving, Hans . . . There were a succession of men who lived in the house. Respectable people didn't speak to my grandmother. All anybody knew about Mother was that she was born at the time when a man from Alsace lived here. He left after two years . . . Mother served at the bar. That's how my father met her . . . Why are you smiling?'

He wasn't smiling. His lips might have stretched a tiny bit, but it was not out of irony. He felt no irony where his aunt was concerned.

He was simply interested . . . What a long journey it had been! . . . That bar, with the woman who had come from somewhere else and her daughter . . . Then Cornelius, a kind of pilgrim who at last put down his bag and moved his tools from the osier field to the back of the shop . . .

'How long did the three of them live together?' he asked.

'Several years. Anna remembers Grandmother. I think she was three when the old lady died. She spent all her time in an armchair in the kitchen because her legs had swollen so much that she couldn't walk any more. Joseph says it was dropsy, and that we still have it in the family . . .'

The grandmother had died, and the atmosphere had started to cleanse itself! The zinc on which drinks were served had been relegated to the far end of the counter. Pure blue signs for Remy Starch, with spotless lions on them, had replaced chromos advertising hard liquor, or even more daring images, on the windows . . .

Aunt Maria was young and beautiful but had probably already acquired that calm, dignified, somewhat rigid demeanour of hers.

'Why didn't they leave?'

As he said it, he found his own question ridiculous.

'Why should they?' Liesbeth replied. 'Where would they have gone? The house was theirs. They were doing a good trade. When the bargees stop here, they stock up for several days . . .'

So of course they had stayed!

They had stayed for no particular reason, just because they were here!

Had Cornelius, for instance, had a reason to stop in this place?

He had travelled through part of Germany, Belgium, northern France. He had reached an osier field between a river and a canal and had settled there, simply, without looking any further, as the Jews had stopped when they reached the Promised Land.

Did he even think of himself as a foreigner? He had kept his long porcelain pipe, his religion, his customs. He spoke the dialect of his home region, in which French words had gradually become embedded, and his nearest and dearest had had to familiarize themselves with his language.

'Mother's never said anything, but I know it was hard . . .'

Hard to stay? To cling to this stretch of canal, this lock, the few walls of the house?

Hard to earn money, surely, in the face of people's hostility! To earn it sou by sou, brick by brick, first to build the upper floors, then to send the children to good schools and dress them respectably, to have a lounge, a piano and shelves filled with honest merchandise!

It wasn't quite the town. It was no longer the country. It was the edge of town, and streets were only just starting to appear, pavements born, streetlamps, the tram line . . .

Other houses came and surrounded the Krull house. A carpenter set up next door. On the other side, office workers and people with small private incomes built houses, people who probably didn't know anything about the grandmother.

All they knew was that the Krulls were foreigners, that they were of no account locally, that they had nothing to do with the neighbourhood but were part of the canal and its itinerant population.

'What about Pipi?' Hans asked.

'I don't know. I've always known her the way she is now. Even when I was little, she was already creating scenes in the shop . . . What are you thinking?'

Without her realizing it, they had become closer. It was one of the rare moments when they were like friends.

A brief moment, because, as she looked at her cousin, Liesbeth gave a shudder. Her body had remembered and had shivered with shame. Her features clouded over.

'If Mother found out . . .' she stammered, bowing her head. 'Why did I do it, Hans? What's going to happen now?'

It didn't happen immediately. They hadn't been paying attention, either of them, to the footsteps on the pavement, then in the shop. The door opened. It wasn't Anna. It was Maria Krull, with her Sunday hat, her silk dress, her jade jewellery, a colourless, expressionless Maria Krull who stood there looking at the two of them.

They couldn't have said what she was thinking, nor if she was surprised or displeased to find them there by the piano. She stared at them, her gaze so deep that she must be seeing something else anyway. And yet she asked in her normal voice, although softly:

'Has your father called me?'

'No, Mother.'

Liesbeth was biting her lip. She had stood up and made a move to rush to her mother, but Maria was already withdrawing, closing the door behind her and setting off up the stairs.

Nothing had happened. Never had an entrance been simpler, or more impressive. Hans frowned, letting the ash drop from his cigarette, unable to respond to his cousin's interrogative look.

Was there a new development? What had the police inspector told Aunt Maria? She didn't have red eyes. She hadn't been crying. And it was even more disturbing to see her so calm, so cold, to hear her toneless voice and those commonplace words:

'Has your father called me?'

Was that all that concerned her, then – keeping her visit to the police station from Cornelius?

Now she was just overhead. They could guess at her every

movement as she undressed, put on her weekday dress and tied her cottonette apron with the tiny blue check pattern around her waist.

'Where are you going, Hans?'

'Nowhere.'

He had had enough of the lounge and the mood they had created there, that was all. He felt like going to see Cornelius, who would be sitting on his chair with the sawn-off legs beside the hunchbacked assistant.

And there he was, his long hands with their prominent veins calmly manipulating the wicker. He raised his head and gave Hans a welcoming look. He had grown accustomed to his nephew coming into the cool workshop from time to time, sometimes sitting down and telling stories about his country.

Hadn't he sensed any of his wife's comings and goings? Hadn't he suspected anything in the morning, when everything had had to be tidied up before he woke?

His long face had its perpetual expression. It was a serene expression, accentuated by his white beard, and yet, at the corners of his lips, you sensed something else at odd moments, a kind of resignation or a secret irony.

'It's hot!' Hans sighed, impressed by the silence and peace of the workshop.

Aunt Maria had already gone back to the shop. She was serving the wife of a bargee, a thin redhead carrying a child on her arm, who had to perform a difficult juggling act to get money out of her big purse.

Then there was another gap, with Anna not daring to say anything and Liesbeth making up her mind, as if in desperation, to do her piano exercises, slowly, harshly, resentfully.

Outside, there was still no sign of Pipi. As for Joseph, he was making so little noise in his room, it was as if he wasn't there.

Several times, Hans felt his aunt's eyes searching him out,

resting on him insistently, but whenever he returned her gaze she would turn away.

For no apparent reason, she had undertaken to rearrange the hundreds of cans of sardines that filled three shelves, and she set about this chore with exaggerated calm and a determination that recalled Liesbeth's staunch application to her piano.

'Lunch is served!' Anna, the only one of the women to show her tiredness, at last announced.

Cornelius arrived from the workshop, and Joseph from upstairs, in his shirtsleeves, weary-eyed.

The quayside was still deserted. It was an open question what had happened to their enemies of the day before and what they were preparing.

Only Germaine, still in her red hat, came to do her usual circuit, like a circus clown. This time, she was accompanied by two girls who were no older than twelve and who were all the more convinced of her importance.

Germaine was walking in the middle, the two others holding on to her arms, just as she had once held on to Sidonie's arm, because she was the oldest.

The three of them formed a compact, hermetic group, whispering terrible secrets and sometimes throwing fearful glances at the Krull house.

But big-breasted Germaine must have been told off the day before after being late for lunch, because the ceremony didn't last, and the cluster of girls set off again, solemn as grown-ups, in the direction of Rue Saint-Léonard.

As for Joseph, he was so pale and weary that it was a pitiful sight, and it was only when he was sure nobody was looking at him that he could bring himself to cast anxious glances at his mother.

'Haven't you finished your thesis yet?' Anna asked him, in

order to bring the reassuring sound of a human voice into the kitchen at least.

'I still have a few pages to write.'

'When are you presenting it?'

'On the 7th.'

'Let's hope Monsieur Schoof will have managed to sort things out with the house!'

That was another story. As soon as he had presented his thesis, Joseph, who had been a non-resident student at a teaching hospital for the past two years, would set up as a doctor.

They had in mind a new little house in that part of the quayside already incorporated into the town. This house was to be Marguerite's dowry: she had chosen it for its spick-and-span appearance and its little garden with a fence around it.

The wedding and the move were due to take place simultaneously in the autumn, but the current owner of the house was demanding a price that Monsieur Schoof considered excessive, and complicated negotiations had been going on for more than a month now.

'Aren't you eating any spinach?'

He shook his head. As for Cornelius, there was a tradition they had never been able to get him to abandon, except when they had company, which was that he used, not one of the knives from the dinner set, but his pocket knife, which he had had for forty years and whose blade was now down to less than a centimetre in width. He would cut his bread on his thumb, bend down and hold his beard with his left hand as he lifted the food to his mouth.

'Do you have a lesson this afternoon, Liesbeth?' Maria Krull asked.

'Yes, at two. A harmony class.'

A plane flew over the neighbourhood, so loudly and so low that you wondered if it was going to knock down a chimney pot or damage a roof, as the newspapers sometimes reported. Joseph was the first to rise from the table and go upstairs.

They still didn't know what had happened in the police inspector's office. Aunt Maria, as she did every day, first helped Anna to wash the dishes.

Was she deliberately delaying the moment? Was she preparing herself, summoning up her strength, practising to maintain the inhuman calm she had been displaying since the morning?

In addition, there was Hans, who didn't know what to do with himself and was always there whenever the others were about to relax.

Didn't Aunt Maria even once throw him an imploring look as she carried out some kind of inspection of the shop?

She tidied, touched this or that thing, opened and closed the till.

At last, she seemed to take a deep breath. Through the half-open door to the kitchen, she announced to Anna:

'I'll be right down!'

She climbed the stairs with calculated slowness, holding her skirts, stopped for a while on the landing and at last turned a door knob. It resisted. She knocked softly.

'Who is it?' came Joseph's voice.

'It's me,' she breathed.

For two hours Anna and Hans were like two caged animals, angry less at being in a cage than at having been thrown together and bumping into each other at every step.

Anna, unusually for her, did nothing, didn't feel up to attempting any chore. Whenever she lost her composure, she went and stood behind the counter as if expecting customers.

That was how Hans observed that she shared her mother's habit of standing on tiptoe and peering out at the quayside, as if clandestinely, above the window display.

Red bricks were being unloaded in the sun, the brightness of the red in stark contrast with the green of the foliage.

But that was a long way away: less than a hundred metres and yet in another world, from which they might have been separated by an unbridgeable gap.

What existed were the voices from upstairs, one very low, the other little more than a whisper: a strange dialogue, consisting first of all of an interminable monologue only punctuated by the occasional rare interjection from Joseph.

The door had been locked. They had also clearly heard the sound of a window being closed.

And all they knew was that Maria Krull was talking, talking, in an even tone, like someone reciting the Bible, like pious women mumbling their rosaries in some dark corner of a church.

'Are you going to keep wandering around the house like that?' Anna finally protested, sick with dizziness.

He didn't reply but threw her a look that was neither spiteful nor ironic. It might not have been affectionate, but for the first time it was imbued with a friendly curiosity.

'What gave you the idea of coming to this house?'

'The fact that I couldn't go anywhere else.'

'If anything happens' (she didn't dare say 'anything bad'!) 'you'll be responsible.'

'Do you think so?'

He took an acid drop from a jar and popped it in his mouth.

'What did the inspector say to you?'

'Nothing . . . Almost nothing.'

And now, after an hour, they heard a noise different from the others, like a body slumping to the floor, but hard: the sound, more or less, that someone would make falling to his knees.

Anna looked at Hans, who didn't move. They both held their breaths.

And now came Joseph's monologue, disjointed, incoherent, interspersed with silences that might have been sobs.

How long did he speak for? Five minutes? Ten? A long time, anyway, long and painful.

Then more noises. It was to be hoped that it was over. There were hurried footsteps, more steps and finally the characteristic creak of bedsprings that had just received the weight of a body.

'Hans!'

He didn't turn.

'Do you know something? Tell me! I'm at the end of my tether! Did Joseph . . .?'

He didn't like Anna, for no reason, perhaps because she wasn't physically exciting, perhaps simply because she didn't like him either, and yet he was moved, searched for an answer and finally stammered:

'Who knows?'

They couldn't cry, any of them! They were under pressure! They would open their mouths to say something and then not utter a word!

What was going on up there? Why the absolute silence? A silence that never ended!

A carter came in, his horsewhip over his shoulder, and said in a familiar tone:

'I'll have a brandy.'

Anna served him but overfilled the glass. She had the presence of mind to grab a cloth and wipe the counter.

Phew! On the first floor, they were finally standing. Joseph was speaking. He only uttered a few sentences. His mother resumed her homily. They sat down again. Now they were conversing more calmly . . .

And Anna, slipping the carter's coins into the metal-lined till and looking out at the quayside, at last summoned up the courage to say:

'The best thing you can do is leave. Apart from anything else, you're going to cause Liesbeth nothing but unhappiness.'

He didn't have time to ask her what she meant by that. The door upstairs opened and closed. Aunt Maria went into her room, but only stayed there for a few moments. At last she came slowly downstairs, crossed the kitchen and stood at the door leading to the shop.

Head tilted slightly to the right, so much like herself that it was incredible, she murmured:

'What are you two plotting?'

8.

It was 6.55. On the rectilinear canal, transformed in places into a tunnel by the foliage joining overhead, a few boats were still moving between the green embankments and the rows of trees, some with engines thudding, others drawn slowly by horses, all bathed in the same peace of the evening, the same oblique pink sun setting ablaze the windows of a white house amid the greenery and casting on the ground the outsized shadow of a little girl leading a dappled percheron.

The engine of the *Centaure* throbbed as it hurried towards the lock at Tilly. The water was split in two. The walls came closer, and the bargee hooted his siren several times, because he could see the lock-keeper, his winch in his hand, walking back to his house.

Shielding his eyes with his hand, the lock-keeper watched the *Centaure* arrive, consulted his big silver watch and at last resigned himself to slowly opening the gates.

It was three reaches upstream of the Krull house, some seven to eight kilometres. The Tilly lock was the least popular with the bargees, because of its oval basin and its side sluices that let out too much water at once and caused eddies.

The family on the *Centaure* wanted to get to the village above the lock by nightfall. The bargee's wife stood in the bow, letting out the steel rope little by little as they advanced.

People had said a hundred times:

'There's going to be disaster at the Tilly lock one of these days! A barge will have to go down before the Highways Department makes up its mind to do something about it!'

The disaster happened. Did the woman let the rope out too fast? The barge was pushed away from the wall by the eddies and advanced at least one metre, enough for its bow to get lodged on the concrete, from which the water was receding.

The woman cried out. The bargee ran to the bow. The lock-keeper bent over, but it was already too late: the *Centaure*, whose bow was almost completely out of the water, was slowly breaking in two.

It was carrying cement.

At the other end of the straight line and the two rows of trees, the Krulls had no inkling of any of this and carried on with their lives as if nothing had happened on the canal.

Just as the accident was taking place, Hans, who had temporarily had enough of the kitchen, the lounge and the shop, was standing at the door of the yard, lighting a cigarette. Throwing away the match, he looked at the low, whitewashed wall that separated the yard from the Guérins' garden. Above the wall, he saw the head of a little boy who was standing there motionless, perched on something or other, a ladder or a barrel, staring at him wide-eyed.

'Louis!' a woman's voice cried.

The boy didn't move. He wanted to keep looking, as if dumb-founded at the sight in front of him.

'Louis! Will you come down? I forbid you to look into those people's house!'

The door to the workshop was open. Cornelius and his assistant must have heard, but neither of them had reacted; nor did they react when Hans sat down beside them.

But there was a mischievous gleam in the assistant's eye, especially when Hans began:

'Did I tell you the story of the monkey? It was when I was

living in Düsseldorf, with a cousin of my mother's who had a perfume shop near the railway station . . .'

The assistant smiled to himself. It was a smile that was peculiar to him, rather like a man eating a sweet. He could have kept score in a notebook of all the relatives or friends in whose homes Hans had lived for a while all over Germany. All his stories started in the same way:

'When I was in Berlin, living with Aunt Marthe . . .'

Or:

'When I was on holiday in the Tyrol, staying with my friends the Von Neumanns . . .'

The assistant would make chewing motions with his mouth, perhaps out of an inner delight at these words, or perhaps because it was a tic.

Apart from the accident at the lock eight kilometres away – but they wouldn't hear about that until the following day – nothing happened that evening, and the Krull household relaxed, weary from being anxious for such a long time.

Nothing but trifles. For example, as they were sitting down at the table, Joseph's chair remained empty, and none of them could help looking at it. Yet they had already called up to him twice from the foot of the stairs that dinner was served.

So Aunt Maria went up, without saying a word. She came down a few moments later and simply announced:

'He's coming.'

And he came. He didn't look at anybody. It was obvious he had been crying, but they pretended not to notice.

Similarly, immediately after the meal, it was Aunt Maria who advised him, as if talking to a sick man:

'Go straight up to bed. It'll do you good.'

Finally, although they were in the habit of closing the shop much later:

'I'll lower the shutters . . .'

Cornelius didn't object, even though it was the moment when he liked to stand in the doorway and smoke a last pipe, watching the air turn blue under the trees.

In short, by the grace of Maria Krull, whose chalky fingers seemed to be brushing away a monstrous spider's web, nothing happened, or rather everything went on as if nothing was happening.

But from time to time, Hans, who, like a woman, sensed much more than he understood, caught a brief glance from his aunt when he was looking somewhere else. It wasn't a glance like the others, like the old ones. She wanted to know what he thought. She was watching him, scrutinizing him. She knew that he knew. He knew that she knew. It was as if the others, the members of the family, now counted much less than Hans the foreigner!

'She'd like to speak to me,' he thought.

'He guesses that I need him!' she told herself.

She had lost all her resentment at the scrounger that he was, all her impatience, just as Hans had lost all his irony. They were each waiting for the other to make a move. But it wouldn't happen this evening. They needed time. Within ten minutes, both were in their rooms.

At this hour, people were strolling casually on the quayside, couples, husbands and wives getting a bit of air or taking their children for a walk, women with little dogs. The red hat went back and forth: Germaine was again accompanied by the same two young girls as at lunchtime.

Presumably because of the hour, and because there were young men about, all three of them adopted a more romantic demeanour, and although they did look towards the Krull house, they didn't cause a scene.

Much later, when Hans was half asleep, other young men

came back from town, singing, and one of them kicked the door, but he might have done it to any of the houses.

Hans, who was sleeping with the window open, was woken by raised voices in the shop. For a moment, he thought Aunt Maria was arguing with someone, but when he listened he realized that the man, a bargee, wasn't angry with her but with the government and in particular the Highways Department.

Noise was coming from the lock, where groups had formed around a handwritten poster announcing that because of the accident at the Tilly lock, the canal would be shut down for a period of about twenty days.

During the night, the waters had already gone down by twenty centimetres, and big bubbles that evoked the idea of illness rose to the surface.

Still at his window, Hans made another discovery. Some fifty metres from the house, a policeman was standing guard, which wasn't customary.

There must have been one there all night, perhaps the previous night, too, although Hans hadn't noticed. That would explain why the girl with the breasts and buttocks had been less demonstrative than before, and also why there hadn't been any more graffiti scrawled on the house.

The officer was in uniform, which meant he wasn't there to keep an eye on the Krulls but to protect them. Clearly, Aunt Maria had lodged a complaint.

Hans washed himself from head to foot in cold water, and Anna got into a temper again because he flooded the waxed floor. He served himself coffee as he did every morning and, through the half-open door, again saw his aunt looking at him conspiratorially.

He knew now that it was going to happen soon. Playing the innocent, he picked up the local newspaper, which was put on the counter every morning, although nobody read it apart from Anna, who was interested in the obituaries.

The mysterious affair of Quai Saint-Léonard.

We have learned that there may well be new developments in the Quai Saint-Léonard case. The man named Potut, who had been arrested following the discovery of the body of Sidonie S—, was released several days ago. It has been confirmed that he is not involved in this terrible crime.

We have reason to believe that the police are currently following another lead which appears to be significant.

Pure chance again, surely! An old reporter from the newspaper who had heard some vague rumours while doing his rounds of the police stations!

Hans closed the newspaper and put it back in its place without saying a word. He was wondering when and how Aunt Maria was going to speak to him, if she would do it quite naturally in the shop, or arrange to see him upstairs, or . . .

He headed for the lounge, which was filled with the din of the piano, and, just as he had done the previous day, passed his hand over the back of Liesbeth's neck, because he loved to repeat the same gestures, search for certain moods he had already enjoyed.

This time, Liesbeth said nothing, leaned her head forwards a little to decipher her score. Just then, Aunt Maria came in, pretending to get an object from a drawer.

Immediately, Liesbeth stood up and went out. She must have been told:

'As soon as you see me with him, leave us alone.'

Just as Anna must have been asked to mind the shop!

So at last they were face to face, in the lounge with its flowered wallpaper and fragile trinkets. Hans noticed that his aunt had put on her glasses, which she generally only used for reading. It wasn't to see him better, but, on the contrary, to hide her eyes from him. Still looking in the drawer, she said without looking at him:

'Have you heard from your father, Hans?'

He remained unruffled. Even though it was a shock, he smiled and almost felt like muttering:

'You clever thing, you!'

He understood. He anticipated that what happened next would be unpleasant, but that didn't stop him from nonchalantly lighting a cigarette, or going to sit on the edge of the table – something his aunt hated.

'I haven't had a letter from him lately,' he replied in a light tone.

'That's a pity. Monsieur Schoof is worried about the poor man.'

'Really?'

She finally abandoned her rummaging in the drawer, which was getting irritating. She remained standing with her back to the window, in her familiar pose, hands folded on her belly.

'Hasn't your father been dead for fifteen years?'

Hans' lips quivered. Yes, this was going to be unpleasant, but he was determined to be a good sport. He decided to laugh, with a tense little laugh.

'Did the inspector tell you? I'd forgotten that he looked at my passport.'

'What are you planning to do, Hans?'

He had to think quickly, feel quickly and above all not make a mistake. Two or three days earlier, in the same circumstances, he would simply have had to leave, as had happened to him in other places where he had settled for a longer or shorter time.

But he remembered the looks his aunt had given him the previous day. He was still watching her closely, convinced that she was playing a game, like a peasant at the market criticizing the cow he is about to buy.

She must have prepared this conversation point by point, as meticulously as if she had written it down. She had started by putting her opponent in a difficult position. But what was her final aim?

'What am I planning to do? Well, aunt, I admit I don't yet know. I have a friend in the south, someone I knew at school, but I'm not sure of his address. All I know is that he lives in a villa between Nice and Cannes . . .'

He was being cynical. He considered that was the best way. He hadn't expected what came next:

'What about Liesbeth?'

'Liesbeth?' he echoed, giving himself time to recover.

What exactly did his aunt know about his relationship with Liesbeth? Who had spoken? Could it have been Joseph, during the long scene the previous day? Had he told her everything? Or else had Anna informed her mother of her still vague suspicions?

'You're not answering.'

What was encouraging in spite of everything was his aunt's attitude: she remained calm, a touch mournful. It wasn't the attitude of a woman who has just learned that she is harbouring a con man, someone who, on top of everything else, has taken wicked advantage of her daughter.

What was it, then?

'I'll do whatever you decide, aunt!' he replied without committing himself.

'Do you realize what you are?'

He brazened it out:

'I realize I've never had any choice, and that my life was bound to work out the way it has.'

It didn't mean anything, but it allowed him to remain

nonchalant, even to look at Maria Krull defiantly. Too bad for her if she took it in that way!

'Listen, Hans . . .'

She had already lowered her voice, and he thought:

'Let's see what her proposition is!'

Because she was going to make one! This scene was meaningless otherwise. His aunt was actually in an even more difficult position than he was. That was why she had put her glasses on, because they gave her self-confidence and prevented the anguish and indecisiveness in her eyes from being obvious.

'Listen to me . . .'

She was still hesitating, looking down at the floor.

'Monsieur Schoof could lodge a complaint. Because of you, because your papers aren't in order and we didn't declare you to the police, we're already going to have to pay a heavy fine, the inspector told me that yesterday. As for Liesbeth, she's a minor, and if there were any consequences . . .'

She had to turn her head away. The vision through her glasses was blurred, because the lenses had steamed up.

'There won't be any!' he hastened to assert.

He was sure of himself. And he really did want to remove any concern she might have on that point.

She, for her part, didn't dare insist.

'Anyway, you have to go . . . You won't even be able to stay in France, because you'll need money, and the inspector told me you won't get a work permit . . .'

These last words irresistibly provoked a smile from Hans, who was no longer embarrassed at all.

'And you realize you won't be able to stay here. Even if nothing had happened, we couldn't have kept you here, doing nothing. We aren't rich . . . People don't look favourably on us . . .'

'I know . . .'

No, that wasn't sufficient. She was insistent, and she must have her reasons. She was speaking slowly, which proved that it was a prepared speech and that she was afraid of losing the thread.

'We may be naturalized, but people treat us as foreigners. If it wasn't for the bargees and the carters, we'd have to close the grocery. You come here straight from Germany and do nothing to pass unnoticed. On the contrary . . .'

He smiled again. It was true! He felt a wicked pleasure in playing the foreigner, in speaking German, in sitting on café terraces and asking for different drinks from other people, and in walking the streets bare-headed in an open-necked shirt, as nobody else in the neighbourhood did.

'What was I saying?'

'That I don't do anything to pass unnoticed.'

She bent down and watched through the window as the woman next door, Madame Guérin, swept her stretch of the pavement and occasionally cast angry glances at the Krull house. She wondered if there had been another incident, but the silence of the shop reassured her.

'You know as well as I do what's happened in the last few days. Whenever anything unpleasant happens, they blame us. When a typhoid epidemic broke out and Joseph caught it like anyone else, the local women said he was the one who'd passed the disease on to everyone.'

Calmly, as if they were discussing business, he stubbed out his cigarette in the ashtray and lit another.

'Because of what happened to that girl, people are again getting worked up against us.'

He blinked at the euphemism. *What happened to that girl!* She meant the attack at the edge of the canal, Sidonie strangled, stripped, raped, thrown in the water . . .

'The inspector has received some anonymous letters. As

long as they haven't found the culprit, some people automatically think it's one of us.'

Her voice was less steady now.

'I realized that the first day. I foresaw everything that's happened and will still happen. We had a quiet day yesterday, but it'll start again and it'll be worse.'

'What did Joseph say?'

He had preferred to go straight on to the attack. Aunt Maria didn't completely lose her composure, but it was clear it had hit home.

'Joseph has nothing to do with that nasty business. I'm sure of it. He swore to me yesterday . . .'

So she, too, had suspected him! Which meant she had been dreading something like that from her son! Obviously, she knew him!

His eyes lowered, Hans was savouring his little victory, and Aunt Maria felt obliged to insist:

'When I left the inspector, I was determined to set my mind at rest. Joseph may have his faults, but he's never lied. I just have to look him in the eyes to know . . . What are you trying to say, Hans?'

Because he had just made a face.

'Nothing, aunt!'

'I repeat, Joseph didn't do anything. Yes, there may be some evidence against him, but it's precisely because he's always been too upright, and perhaps because we brought him up too strictly.'

She sniffled, almost took her handkerchief from the pocket of her apron, but resisted, because it would have been almost an admission of defeat.

'What evidence?'

'Stupid things. Kids like that girl with the red hat who let their imagination run riot.'

'I suppose she said Joseph was following Sidonie and her that evening at the fair.'

'These girls always imagine men are following them. It doesn't matter, Hans! What matters is what people think. The inspector knows how much credit to give malicious gossip like that.'

'Do you think so?'

'He told me so himself.'

'Well, what I think is that he's carrying out a thorough investigation.'

He almost went to fetch the morning paper and show his aunt the revealing item.

'That's neither here nor there!' she insisted. 'They can do all the investigating they want, they won't find anything against Joseph, nothing of importance anyway. What scares me is the local people. They'll make our lives unbearable . . . Unless . . .'

A silence. She had finally reached the culmination of this talk and suddenly she felt dizzy and rushed awkwardly towards the conclusion.

'Since you have to leave anyway, you might as well go abroad straight away, to Germany or elsewhere. If you slip out of town quietly, they're sure to suspect you . . .'

Her chest swelling with hope beneath her corset, she was looking at him with all her might, as if to cast a spell on him, to drag a 'yes' from him.

'You have nothing to lose! Once across the border . . .'

So this was what she had been building towards! Hans, who wasn't easily surprised, was nevertheless stunned. He admired his aunt, who had put together this whole speech just in order to say to him:

'We could have you put in prison for fraud. You took advantage of Liesbeth. You've disrupted our house, but none of that matters if you agree to be the scapegoat and take suspicion away from Joseph!'

It made Joseph, for whom she had devised this plan, seem bigger somehow. And all this time he had been upstairs, by his open window, bent over his exercise books!

In the kitchen, Anna and Liesbeth were waiting.

'I know these people, I'm sure they'll leave us alone,' she concluded in a muted voice, turning towards the window.

And the word *people*, which endlessly recurred in her speeches and in the conversations in the house, assumed a particular resonance among the Krulls, an almost fearsome significance. *People* meant the rest of mankind, the living ocean that surrounded the island of the family. It began with the Guérins and extended to the limits of the world.

'People will leave us alone . . .'

In other words, the storm would move away with Hans . . .

'What exactly did Joseph tell you, aunt?'

He was no longer the accused. He no longer needed to brazen it out. On the contrary, it was he who now asked the questions in an incisive tone.

'Look, Hans . . .'

His aunt pointed beyond the tulle curtain, out to the quay-side and the lock where the idle bargees seemed quite agitated again. Among them, the vulgar figure of Pipi could be seen, holding forth. It was as if they could hear her voice. They guessed that she was telling a new audience all about her daughter. From time to time she would stretch her arm out in the direction of the Krull house.

'I can see.'

'They'll even end up blaming us for the fact that the canal's been shut down! Whereas if you leave . . .'

'What did Joseph confess to you?'

'Why should he have confessed anything?'

'Because he cried, because he threw himself on his knees in front of you then, I assume, had a fit of hysterics and lay down on his bed.'

She said nothing.

'He knew Sidonie, didn't he?'

'He'd spoken to her twice in the street. It was her friend who told the inspector. She says they both made fun of him because he was awkward around women.'

'And that night?'

'What's the matter, Hans? Why are you looking at me like that?'

'Because I want to know!'

'Do you think—?'

'I don't think anything! I know Joseph isn't a man like any other. I have an idea what he got up to in the street at night. Before this thing happened, he used to go out every night, didn't he?'

'He went out for air!'

'And he didn't have any friends, not even at the university.'

'Because he's always shunned for being German!'

'He didn't have a girlfriend either.'

'He's too shy . . .'

She was answering reluctantly and felt angry with herself for doing so. He remained seated in a nonchalant pose on the corner of the table, creasing an embroidered doily.

'What else did he tell you?'

'Nothing, I assure you . . . Why must you insist?'

She was looking at the door, the ceiling. You might have thought she was going to call her son to the rescue.

'You have to understand, aunt, that I'm no idiot. We were together when we passed a couple embracing under a street-lamp, and I saw him. His hands started shaking. For a while, he couldn't speak. And it has the same effect on him when he walks behind a woman who's probably almost naked under her dress, or looks up at a window and sees a woman's silhouette behind the blind . . . I had a friend, in Germany—'

'Be quiet, Hans!'

'With this friend, it was the sight of a leg. And until he was finally able to—'

'Hans!'

'I bet Joseph hid in dark corners to watch couples kissing . . .'

She had to sit down, and this time she did take her handkerchief from her pocket, but only to mop her brow.

'He didn't kill her,' she said. 'He swore to me—'

'Then why is he so scared?'

She gave him a long look that was in no way like those that had preceded it. She was pretty much defeated. She seemed to be asking him:

'Can I trust you?'

Because the unlikeliest thing was happening: Aunt Maria, mistrust incarnate, was falling under Hans' influence.

'He told me everything,' she stammered at last. 'He did follow her. He wanted to talk to her again, but without her friend, who made fun of him. He admitted to me that he was attracted by the girl because, like him, she was tubercular . . .'

Hans was listening, as solemn as a doctor.

'It wasn't until they got to the quayside that he noticed someone else was following her, a stocky man in a felt hat . . .'

'Go on, aunt!'

She had to break off to cry a little, out of weariness even more than because she was upset. She looked up at him imploringly.

'Why do you want—'

'What did he see?'

'It's my fault! If I'd let him go with girls, like any other man, it wouldn't have happened. But I was only thinking of his health! When he was small, he couldn't adapt to things. At school he was always ill and—'

'He hid, didn't he?'

'The man had accosted the girl and was talking to her. Apparently at first she didn't seem to be pushing him away, then she went right to the edge of the canal with him. It was near a pile of bricks that's still there. They kissed. The man became more forward, and the girl struggled . . .'

What words had Joseph used to describe this scene to his mother?

'They both rolled on the ground . . . He didn't see him strangle her. He thought . . .'

'And he stayed to the end?'

'By the time he realized, it was too late, and the man was dragging the body to the canal. Joseph didn't see his face. According to him, he looked like a vagrant. He was dressed like the tramps you see wandering the countryside.'

'What about the anonymous letters?'

'It's the same old story. Girls telling their parents Joseph followed them, or had spoken to them. You could say the same of all the young men. If Joseph admits to the police that he was there . . . Hans! You've already done us a lot of harm. My poor Liesbeth, from now on . . .'

She wept a little more.

And speaking into her handkerchief, which distorted her voice:

'You have to save Joseph. You have to, do you hear? You have to leave here, so that people will stop bothering us.'

For a moment he thought Aunt Maria was going to get down on her knees, as Joseph had done the previous day.

Just then, a bargee in clogs clumped into the shop.

9.

How had Maria Krull known that those steps were not the honest steps of a customer but that they constituted a threat? It had only taken a few stomps of the man's clogs on the floor for her to abandon one drama for another and listen out carefully. Her gaze became sharper, and she forgot about Hans; in her mind she was already running towards the shop, and now her body followed her mind. Hans was never to forget that image of her, as heavy and definitive as a photograph in a family album: she had reached the kitchen and was standing against one half of the glass door. This door had a thin curtain over it, and the light made a halo around her grey hair, while her face was more moulded, firmer against the light.

The other half of the door was ajar, and Aunt Maria, head bent, was watching the enemy, ready to rush to Anna's rescue.

The man was a bargee they had seen a few moments earlier move away from the group being stirred up by Pipi. Already at the school in his village he must have been a braggart, always looking for applause and laughter, defying the teacher like a proud idiot.

'You'll see!' he had said to them, his moustache damp, his eyes gleaming.

And as he crossed the central reservation, he was all puffed up from knowing they were watching him and turned from time to time to make sure, making a little sign as if to say to the gallery:

'Don't worry! You'll see!'

But as he got closer to the shop he slowed down, so that he came in more or less at the speed of an ordinary customer.

Anna was behind the counter. Liesbeth was in a corner of the shop, in order not to remain alone in the kitchen or in her room. Both were pale, anxiety written all over their faces.

'What can I get you?' Anna nevertheless asked, suspecting nothing.

She was surprised to see the policeman, who usually stayed fifty or a hundred metres away, come and stand just outside the window and look through it.

'A Pernod!'

Anna looked among the bottles. It was then that Aunt Maria took up her position behind the door.

His drink served, the gleaming idiot grabbed it, gave Anna a mocking look, flung the liquid across the shop and put the glass back down on the counter.

He was pleased! He looked Anna in the eyes, proud of himself for challenging a young woman, wiped his moustache and at last said:

'I don't feel like drinking in a murderer's house!'

Anna automatically turned her head to the kitchen and saw her mother in the doorway. Did the man also see her? Whether he did or not, he headed for the shop door. Just outside, the policeman hesitated, then merely said:

'Be on your way. We don't want trouble.'

At what point had Hans gone upstairs? It was hard to be sure. He always came and went without making a noise, without stirring the air. Realizing that he wasn't in the kitchen or the lounge, Maria Krull went to the foot of the stairs and heard him quietly turning the handle of Joseph's door.

Hans wasn't deliberately trying to surprise anyone. The door didn't creak. His soles came to rest silently on the floor.

It was he who was surprised at the silence in the room. For a moment he took it for emptiness. On the table by the window, an exercise book lay open beside a bottle of green ink and a pen holder with a chewed end. But there was nobody on the chair, nobody in this part of the room, where the green trees outside were reflected in the mirrored wardrobe and the hands of a black marble clock had been frozen for ages at ten to twelve.

Joseph was there, though, lying fully clothed on his bed, looking taller than ever, his big feet in yellow slippers. One of his hands was dangling to the floor, to the rug with the red background, his mouth was open, and his breathing was regular.

It was the only corner of the house with a male smell, a smell of sweat and cold tobacco. As he passed, Hans glanced automatically at the exercise book, its pages covered in Joseph's small handwriting. A title was written in a rounded hand:

Anatomical type: lesions

But there was as yet nothing below it, just finger marks, worn paper over which a man must have sat for a long time, stubbornly, thinking about something else. In the margin, Joseph had finally written, in pencil, in different handwriting: *It might be enough to slap a policeman in the street, or lie without blushing, or . . .*

It ended with a drawing that depicted nothing, one of those complicated doodles you draw when your mind is elsewhere.

Then he had gone and laid his dismal body on the bed without removing the counterpane. Had he slept much during the last few nights? Probably not. But now sleep had finally taken him, a heavy diurnal sleep. His white shirt, open at the neck, was wet.

There was a chair near the bedside table and Hans sat down on it and gazed at his cousin. He didn't move. He made no sound and yet, from deep in his numb sleep, Joseph was aware of an alien presence and he came slowly back to the surface, a shudder ran over his damp skin, his Adam's apple moved up and down, and at last sight filtered through his eyelashes.

When he recognized Hans, he made an effort to wake more quickly, rubbing his face with his hands.

'What do you want?' he asked in a thick voice.

Hans smiled unwittingly. It wasn't a smile, strictly speaking, but something very light, a touch of pity, a very small touch of irony.

Joseph folded his big body in two. His feet touched the floor. For a moment, he sat there on the edge of the bed.

'Are you happy now?'

With the best will in the world, Hans couldn't have explained why there was still that faint glimmer of gaiety on his face, like a reflection of the morning, the pale sky, the clear air stretching to infinity beyond the window, full of sounds and life.

He had just seen Joseph asleep. Now he saw him barely awake, timid and sly. He couldn't help saying to him:

'Idiot!'

He couldn't take his eyes off his cousin. It was a prodigious spectacle, watching Joseph get up, worried, jealous, bitter, and understanding everything that was happening inside him, the slightest movements, even those that Joseph himself was unaware of!

That was the extraordinary thing: Hans could have been Joseph! He was capable of being both Joseph and Hans! He could have played both parts himself, said both men's lines in the dialogue that was about to start.

While Joseph was only Joseph!

He was standing, his head higher than the light hanging over the table. His face was still shiny from the sweat of sleep, and the back of his shirt was crumpled.

'I've just had a long conversation with Aunt Maria,' Hans began, standing up and going to the window.

He sat down on the sill and lit a cigarette.

'What did my mother tell you?'

'Everything! She'd like me to leave here so that people will suspect me. She reckons that way the family will be left alone. How stupid is that?'

Joseph, head bowed, said in a muffled voice:

'They have no right to bother us! I didn't do anything.'

If he had been less tall, the sight would have been less pitiful. But he was huge, and his head, when he lowered it that way, seemed to hang at the end of his long neck.

Until now, in his relations with Hans, what had dominated was hatred and suspicion. The hatred of someone who feels inferior and can't stand feeling it, who considers that inferiority to be an injustice but is unable to react against it.

A hatred based on unwilling admiration, on envy!

And now, today, faced with a Hans who knew everything and was dominating him with his Olympian smile, he was reduced to stammering:

'I didn't do anything . . .'

'That's the most ridiculous part of it!'

Hans couldn't keep the sarcasm out of his voice. Looking outside, he saw Pipi move away from the group and start towards the house.

Joseph was struggling with himself, struggling to overcome his timidity, his meekness, his jealous admiration for his cousin's nonchalant, cynical attitude.

'Since I didn't kill that girl . . .'

'You're the one they suspect and will continue to suspect.'

There was a new familiarity in the way he addressed Joseph. He wasn't being contemptuous, or superior. They had suddenly got closer.

'Because I'm a foreigner!' Joseph retorted. 'It's always the same! Every time something happens in the neighbourhood, they blame us.'

Hans was both inside and outside. He was following Pipi with his eyes and imagining Aunt Maria's forehead and grey hair as she watched the enemy over the window display.

But he still kept his eyes on Joseph as he gradually freed himself from the slackness of sleep.

'It's not because you're foreigners,' he said in the tone of a man who knows the truth and is unassailed by doubt. 'It's because you're not foreign enough! Or else because you're too foreign.'

They heard the bell ring in the shop. Liesbeth and Anna were probably in the kitchen, looking through the tulle curtain. The policeman moved closer to the window.

'We're not foreign enough?' Joseph echoed with a frown.

'Or too much! You're not honest about being foreign. You're shamefaced foreigners. Just as you're shamefaced Protestants. You come and settle among people and try to be like them. You imitate them clumsily, knowing you'll never be them. And they sense it. I bet you put out more flags than anyone else on the 14th of July, I bet you scatter rose petals in the street on Corpus Christi. People resent you for it more than if you did nothing at all, than if you quite boldly closed your shutters.'

He was silent for a moment. He could hear nothing. It pained him to be missing part of the show, not knowing what was going on between his aunt and Pipi.

'If we were aggressive, it'd be even worse!' Joseph objected.

He was almost cowed. As long as this wasn't just about him,

he could regain his composure and reflect on the ideas put forward by Hans.

'It's not about being aggressive, but about being sure of yourself! Like the Jews when they settle somewhere . . . They aren't ashamed of their names, or their noses. Nor are they ashamed of their business sense, their love of money. That's the way it is and no other way! Never mind what other people think! They keep themselves to themselves and don't care if children in the street make faces at them.'

He gave a start. The bell had just rung again. The policeman could no longer be seen outside in the street. He had come into the shop. The door was still open. They heard him say with feigned severity:

'That's enough now. Don't stay here!'

'She started it!' Pipi squealed. 'She dared to bring up the baby clothes she gave me when my poor daughter was born. They were all worn, she'd already used them for her three children.'

'Come on, just leave! I don't want any trouble.'

'So I'm the one causing trouble now, am I?'

The policeman took her away, and she continued arguing all down the street. Hans looked at his cousin.

'You see!'

'What?'

'Always the same thing! Your mother whined about her good deeds! She's good enough to give, but not enough to forget it. You people are too much and not enough.'

The most extraordinary thing was that he was unwittingly being recognized as having the right to judge them! Joseph was listening to him! Joseph, who the previous day had wanted to throw him out, was having a debate with him!

True, he sneered:

'In other words, we should be completely dishonest!'

'That's best! Or completely honest. But don't lurk on the quayside at night, creeping about, watching couples kissing in the hope of glimpsing a bit of skin . . .'

Joseph turned his head away and cracked his long fingers. He hesitated, and finally said:

'And what about my sister?'

'Liesbeth?' Hans said innocently.

'Yes, Liesbeth.'

He was again overcome with emotion, the same dubious, unhealthy emotion that made his hands shake whenever certain subjects came up.

'Liesbeth is perfectly happy!' Hans asserted.

'Now maybe, but what about later?'

'She'll probably get married one day, and it won't matter any more.'

'Married?'

'Married and all the rest.'

'And what if her husband finds out?'

Hans shrugged, threw his cigarette into the street, lit another and watched as the policeman returned on his own after getting rid of Pipi.

It must have been about eleven in the morning. The hammers from the Rideau boatyard were beating at a rapid pace, and the trams were stopping every three minutes.

Joseph didn't know what else to say, or what attitude to adopt. Nor did he know what to make of his cousin, whom he kept looking at surreptitiously and whose self-confidence he so admired.

He was heavy-hearted. If he could, he would have wept, not only with sadness but with disgust at himself and everything, people, life, what he had done and what he would have liked to do, disgust at being, as Hans had said, too much or not enough . . .

There was a terrible, depressing injustice about it: always, as far back as he could remember, he had wanted to do the right thing, he had always made an effort to be like everyone else, better than everyone else, to be the best student at school, a well-behaved, respectful child at home, to keep his clothes clean, to overcome his worst instincts . . .

And now here he was, in the position of an accused man, while this Hans, who was the same age as him, looked at him with a mocking eye, outshone him with all his calm cynicism.

He felt like bait at the end of a line. It seemed to him that Hans was following his thoughts step by step, ready to reel him in just when he wanted.

He couldn't hate him any more. He could only be subject to him. He was almost at the point where he might ask him for advice!

'Why did you tell your mother all that?' Hans asked, looking around the room as if reconstructing the previous day's scene.

'The inspector had told her . . .'

'What?'

'Everything!'

'What exactly?'

'All about these girls I sometimes followed at night. I was never capable of accosting them. I didn't know what to say to them. I was afraid they'd burst out laughing as soon as I opened my mouth.'

'And now?'

'What do you mean, now?'

'What are you going to do?'

Hans looked his cousin straight in the eyes. It wasn't that he was sorry for him, but he understood, he was thinking, making an effort to play both roles, to feel like Joseph, to anticipate his reactions.

'When the inspector questions me, I'll tell him the truth!'

'Then you're done for!'

He had used the German word: *kaputt!*

'Why?'

'Because they won't believe you.'

Hans had no desire to see this conversation come to an end. He felt fine, sitting there on his window-sill, a ray of sunshine on his back.

And Joseph, for his part, would have been disorientated if his cousin had suddenly left him to his own devices. In the past few minutes, ever since Hans had entered the room, something had changed. Joseph was no longer alone with his shame, his remorse, his rage, his indignation, with all these thoughts and feelings that had been eating away at him for several days.

What was soothing was that, with Hans, words took on a different, almost ethereal meaning, facts were no longer so blunt, even ceased to matter. At a push, they could have talked calmly about Sidonie and the way the drama had unfolded!

'They won't believe you because it isn't plausible. People think a young man should have girlfriends and not be content with just watching. When you watched me with your sister through the keyhole . . .'

Joseph dared to raise his eyes, waiting for the question.

'I bet you weren't all that angry, were you?'

Hans was being benevolent. It was he who decided if things were good or bad, shameful or not. He juggled with them, just as he juggled with his cigarette, moving it from one corner of his lips to the other, so that it constantly looked as if it was going to fall.

'To be honest, you're a little bit disgusting . . . Your mother, too, when it comes down to it, because she knows I slept with her daughter and yet she's asking me to do her a service.'

Joseph didn't object. There was no way out now. Having accepted certain phrases, certain judgements, he was forced to endure the rest.

'You're all weird people, believe me, and if I were one of the locals I wouldn't look kindly on you either. Aunt Maria lectures Pipi but serves her drinks. I mean, if there wasn't anyone to serve her alcohol, Pipi wouldn't be able to get drunk!'

What must they be thinking downstairs? Just like the day before, when Aunt Maria was in this same room with Joseph, Liesbeth and Anna were probably looking up at the ceiling from time to time, wondering what drama was being played out up here.

But there wasn't any drama at all. There was just a plain young man's bedroom. There was Joseph walking up and down, bending his head each time in order to avoid knocking the light, stopping every now and again to face his cousin.

And Hans talking . . .

Yes, he was still talking, in a low voice, letting the words flow as they came to him, as Joseph inspired them.

'Are you going to marry Marguerite?'

Oh, yes! Marguerite and the little house Monsieur Schoof would buy them!

A smart, shiny cage from which Joseph would look out at everything he desired!

And he desired everything!

Just like Hans.

But if Hans desired something, he took it! He had even desired to live in a house like this one, for as long as he could, to sniff its good smells, scandalize Anna, frighten Aunt Maria, push Joseph over the edge, make love with Liesbeth and teach her the most obscene practices.

He had desired it and he had done it!

And when he desired to go somewhere else . . .

'You see, Joseph, in my opinion you'll always be unhappy.'

Joseph blew up. 'Because I'm not like the others! Because I'm a foreigner everywhere! Because I feel different! Because I don't have a country, don't have compatriots, don't have people who think the way I do! Because I was born in a kind of island, and my family are incapable of understanding me. Could I tell my father . . .?'

Hans smiled. The idea of telling old Cornelius these stories about girls was amusing.

Joseph was amusing, too, with his monumental good faith, his obsessive sense that he was a kind of pariah, his hunger to conform, his need to fit into a given order, to feel part of the crowd and be approved by it.

'Ever since kindergarten I've stood out.'

'In my case, it's deliberate!' Hans asserted.

'What is?'

'Trying to be different from the others! That's why people respect me. If I'd come and asked you all nicely to take me in, admitting that I didn't have a cent and didn't know what to do . . . Or if I'd told Liesbeth she was pretty and I was in love with her instead of just throwing her on the bed . . .'

He had turned.

'Ah, there's the other one!' he observed.

The 'other one' was Germaine, still in her awful red hat. Someone else who took herself seriously, who thought her time had come! Barely had she left her shoe shop than she press-ganged one friend or another and came here to keep an eye on the Krulls!

Because in a way they belonged to her. It was thanks to her testimony that an investigation into them had been started. She savoured her own importance, rolling her big buttocks like an older woman, roaring with laughter like a whore, walking up and down in front of the house, whispering God knows what in her companions' ears.

Sidonie was dead, and she had inherited not only her place but the duty to avenge her! She had also inherited young friends with spindly legs who clung to her arms and to whom she imparted more or less accurate information about men and love.

'I bet you would have been capable of following her, too, just like Sidonie,' Hans said, still on the window-sill. 'What this one needs is a good spanking. I might decide to give her one myself!'

He burst out laughing, seeing the face his cousin made at this prospect.

'No, Joseph, don't get so excited as soon as I mention a woman's behind!'

More than ever, Joseph was on the verge of crying. His hands had shaken. He had turned red. He was in a state of confusion. He wanted to beg Hans to leave right now but might just as easily have held him back.

He was afraid of him and he needed him. Since the two of them had been in this room, since the words they had exchanged had begun to disperse the fog, to make the anguish fade, to make complicated ideas disarmingly simple, he had been dreading solitude.

He wasn't defeated, though. He kept looking at his cousin, searching for arguments against him, forcing himself to hate him in spite of everything.

They had both forgotten the three women downstairs, as well as Cornelius in his workshop with the assistant.

The room had almost become a real student's room. Hans threw his cigarette end on the floor and shrugged, his eyes still on Germaine out there.

'Once people start taking themselves seriously . . .' he began.

He broke off, saw Joseph expecting him to continue.

'Well?'

'Nothing. I don't think it's worth it . . .'

It was he, Hans, who had hesitated and was now staring at a point on the floor.

Once people start taking themselves seriously . . . What

then? Why was it his turn to feel queasy? Why had he mentioned the little house that Monsieur Schoof intended for
Joseph and Marguerite?

'But there are things we're obliged to take seriously all the
same!' Joseph sighed. 'Having an affected lung, for instance . . .'

They pricked up their ears. They had just heard, or rather
sensed, the rustle of a skirt on the stairs. There was someone
behind the door. The handle was turning.

'So this is where you are?' Aunt Maria said, looking first at
one then at the other.

She found it hard to conceal her surprise – or was it anxiety?
She probably hadn't expected to find such an atmosphere in her
son's room.

Hans had both feet up on the window-sill, presenting his
profile. Joseph had his elbows on the mantelpiece, near the
clock that still showed ten to twelve.

And both were solemn, with a solemnity that had nothing
tragic about it, the solemnity of young men calmly setting the
world to rights.

Indeed, Joseph looked at his mother in surprise, as if notic-
ing certain things for the first time.

'What's the matter?' he asked.

'Nothing. I just came to see if the two of you were ready for
lunch. It's half past twelve.'

She would have liked to know. She looked from one to the
other. She couldn't get much from her son's face. Joseph was
stubbornly inscrutable, although much calmer than usual.

She fell back on Hans, as if he were her accomplice, and waited
for a gesture from him, some sign that would reassure her.

Hans was looking outside, refusing to answer her appeal.

'Will you come down now?'

'We're coming,' Joseph said.

His mother glanced at the bed. She asked again, in surprise:

'Were you sleeping?'

'I had a little rest.'

She really had the impression she was an intruder. She retreated.

'Come down,' she repeated.

They let her go, listening to her steps diminish on the stairs. Joseph tried to meet his cousin's eyes.

'We really have to do something,' he said in a hesitant voice.

He, too, was waiting for an answer, but obtained only an evasive gesture. Before going down, Hans went over to the exercise book, still open at the same page, and pointed at the words written in the margin:

It might be enough to . . .

He gave a gentle smile that was almost entirely devoid of irony.

They went downstairs, one behind the other.

And when they took their places at the table, the three women looked at them with a degree of anxiety, as if sensing that there was a new bond between them that excluded the rest of the household, that perhaps united them against it.

Cornelius was already eating, holding his beard with his left hand.

10.

It was the first time in quite a while that there had been such a sense of familiarity and routine in the kitchen. Joseph was eating quite naturally and, after not daring to look at the others for several days, now threw curious glances at Anna, Liesbeth and his father, as if he had been away.

Today, there was sauerkraut, which was pure chance, because they rarely made it, and it would play a role in what was to happen.

Aunt Maria and Anna had begun a conversation about the dress the latter wanted to make herself.

'Two metres sixty in width should be enough.'

'I'll need twice that in length, Mother. And if I want to make the skirt a bit wider . . .'

The samples were on the table between the two women, small pieces of bright fabric. Liesbeth had fingered them for a long time, holding them up to the light.

She was barely thinking about what Joseph and Hans might have been discussing for so long.

Just then, the shop door opened, and the bell rang. Aunt Maria looked up, as did Hans, who was again on the same side of the table as her.

As soon as they had peered through the curtain, they exchanged glances. The others noticed and now also looked.

Anna was already pushing back her chair, but Aunt Maria announced:

'I'll go!'

Of the two men who had come in, one was the police inspector. Today, he was wearing a boater and a silky alpaca jacket. Short and fat, he was the perfect image of the petit bourgeois who strolls along the riverbanks watching the anglers fishing.

His companion was the same physical type, although less plump and more surly, perhaps because he suffered with his stomach and liver.

Both men were at their ease. When Maria Krull entered, the inspector had just uncorked a bottle he had taken from the counter and was sniffing it. Simply out of curiosity! He gave the impression that he had told his companion:

'You'll see what a strange shop it is and what strange people they are!'

It was as if he were in a foreign country, finding everything extraordinary, even the banality of it.

'What can I do for you?'

'I'm sorry to disturb you, Madame Krull. This gentleman is the chief inspector from headquarters. He's been put in charge of the investigation into the case you're familiar with. As he has a few questions to ask your son . . .'

Through the curtain, they could see the family frozen around the table.

'So it's my son you want to speak to?' Aunt Maria said suspiciously.

The two men signalled to each other. The chief inspector, the one with stomach problems, took a paper from his pocket and handed it to Madame Krull without a word.

'What's this?'

'Read it!'

'I don't have my glasses.'

'It's a search warrant.'

'What do you want to search?'

'Your son's room, to start with.'

It took her a second to recover. Then she made up her mind and rushed to the door opening on to the corridor.

'Come this way, gentlemen. I'll tell my son. Please, go into the lounge.'

A lounge that was nothing out of the ordinary. Wallpaper with little flowers, shelves with trinkets, some in spun glass, an embroidered table runner, a piano . . .

And yet the two inspectors kept sniffing as if they had discovered an unknown country and, because of the sauerkraut, the man with the bad stomach declared:

'It stinks of Krauts here!'

The first person Aunt Maria looked at when she came back into the kitchen wasn't Joseph, it was Cornelius. But Cornelius, as if he hadn't heard anything, wiped his mouth, calmly stood up, walked over to the rack and took down his long porcelain pipe.

'It's someone for you, Joseph. I showed them into the lounge. Maybe you should put on a jacket . . .'

Joseph got to his feet, much more calmly than might have been expected, and briefly glanced around the family table, as if to fix a complete living image of it in his mind.

They saw him disappear into the lounge but couldn't say anything because Cornelius was still in the kitchen.

They had to wait. Normally, it would be ten or twelve minutes before he went back to his workshop. Did he realize that he was in the way? He didn't say anything. Stepping softly, his pipe between his teeth, he preferred to walk out into the yard.

The door to the lounge was already opening. Joseph was saying:

'This way. I'll lead you.'

There was the clatter made by the three men on the stairs, then on the first floor.

Liesbeth was trying in vain to catch Hans' eye to ask him what was happening. Anna, resigned, had started washing the dishes. Aunt Maria had disappeared.

Hans lingered long enough to light a cigarette then left in his turn, climbed the stairs four steps at a time and opened a door he had never opened before, the door to his uncle's and aunt's room.

He knew that it communicated with Joseph's room. He hadn't taken two steps before he saw Aunt Maria standing against the communicating door, her finger to her lips.

Taking care that the floorboards didn't creak, he moved over to that door, and she left him a little space beside her, their faces almost touching.

'. . . the clothes you were wearing on the 17th . . .'

Joseph replied, opening the mirrored wardrobe:

'These are the only ones I have . . .'

Two grey suits, the same steel-grey, too big for him, giving him that long, slack figure, that irresolute demeanour.

'What day do you do the laundry in this house?'

They recognized the voice of the chief inspector, while the other inspector, the plump one, had sat down on the window-sill, his back to the quayside, in the same pose as Hans that morning.

'Monday,' Joseph replied.

It was startling to hear how normal his voice was, even though he was alone with two police officers.

'Obviously,' one of them muttered, having fingered the grey suits thoroughly.

Which meant there was nothing, that he had expected to find nothing.

Between Hans' nose and his aunt's there wasn't even a gap of ten centimetres. Around them was a room that Hans didn't yet know, the most solid, most permanent in the house, a room in which the smallest object had taken months or years to find its place.

It was in this room that Joseph had been born. It was the same then as it was now! And all his childhood, all his adolescence, he had seen nothing but motionless, eternal things, furniture that had existed for so long that it had lost all sense of men's work, or of material sawn or planed, furniture that was *the* bed, *the* wardrobe, *the* sideboard, *the* armchair where father sat . . .

'I still have a few questions to ask you . . . Sit down if you like.'

Hans imagined the man taking a little piece of paper from his pocket, and he wasn't wrong. The chief inspector had kept his soft hat on his head. It was the time of day he dreaded, immediately after lunch, and every now and again he grimaced in pain.

'Do you know a man named Cloasquin?'

They were leaving the sphere of what Hans knew, but he saw his aunt grow pale at the name and restrain an angry impulse.

Wasn't the name itself like a kind of threat? Cloasquin! Émile Cloasquin!

Joseph's hands had shaken. 'I knew him at school,' he replied.

'The school you were expelled from, I think?'

And the chief inspector, after looking at his piece of dirty paper, went on:

'You hated Cloasquin, whose parents had a grocery on Place Saint-Léonard. He was smaller and weaker than you. You stalked him for weeks and one evening, as he passed a patch of waste ground, you threw yourself at him, knocked him down, pinned him to the ground with your knee on his chest and put your hands round his throat.'

'I was eleven years old!' Joseph said, and they were surprised to hear his voice.

'After that incident, Cloasquin developed jaundice and was confined to his bed for a month, which put his schoolwork back by a year.'

A strange, puny boy, with very fair hair, a mouth that was too big and very small eyes.

'He used to stir all the others up against me, calling me a Kraut . . .'

It was true. The sickly Cloasquin, sure of having all his classmates with him, had taken it out on Joseph, who was nearly a head taller than any of them. Every break time, he would taunt him.

For months, Joseph had suffered patiently, then, as the chief inspector had just said, he had stalked his enemy, laid him low and squeezed his throat, repeating:

'Say sorry! I want you to say sorry and promise to leave me alone.'

'I note just one thing,' the man with the bad stomach recited calmly. 'That you grabbed him by the throat and he fainted. You were eleven, Monsieur Krull!'

A silence. Hans could see Aunt Maria's eye very close to his, the skin of her cheek, every pore of it, as if through a magnifying glass.

'Another thing . . .'

The piece of paper was again called to the rescue.

'Do you know a woman called Marcotte?'

No reply. Had Joseph flinched? This time, Aunt Maria didn't understand, and waited curiously for what would come next.

'You don't deny it, then? You know the woman, you know she solicits on the corner of Rue des Carmes every night. You've approached her on several occasions – quite regularly, in fact, unless I'm mistaken.'

The remarkable thing was that Joseph was much calmer, much more at ease with these two aggressive men than with his mother or even with Hans. He was watching his enemy, the man in the soft hat, in no hurry to answer, waiting to hear the accusations.

'Marcotte has stated that you didn't ask for quite the same thing as the others. Usually, she takes her clients to her place in Impasse des Forgerons. But you always refused to go with her. You insisted on doing it outside, in a dark corner. And this was on every occasion! . . . Shall I read you her statement?'

'There's no need.'

'You admit it?'

A nod. Joseph was still standing. He wasn't defying them. He wasn't blushing either. He just seemed to be thinking, trying to guess where they were going with this.

'Next! Do you know Jeanne Aubray?'

He made an effort and finally murmured:

'I don't recognize the name.'

'She's the maid at the Rideaus'.'

A gorgeous girl, who always went around with the top of her blouse open and turned all the men's heads.

'Three times a week, Jeanne Aubray sees her boyfriend on the quayside, not far from her employers' house. Is it correct that every time they met you hid in a corner to watch, and the boyfriend, who was a stonemason, had to chase you away and threaten to give you a thrashing if you continued to snoop on them?'

No reply. Joseph was tacitly admitting it. Hans could still see Aunt Maria's motionless eye.

'That's not all. Let's get to Sidonie . . . Her friend Germaine was with her when you first approached her. It was a rainy evening. You'd been following the two girls for a long time. They laughed, knowing you were behind them. They did an abrupt about-turn, and you were thrown for a moment and lost your composure. Then you showed them a fifty-franc note you had in your hand . . . Is that correct?'

No reply. The other inspector was smoking his pipe and examining the young man with his large, amused eyes.

'This wasn't the only time you did this with young girls. You always showed them money.'

Joseph sounded distant but clear, although glum.

'Because I didn't dare talk to them!'

'In other words, you didn't want to flirt with them like other young men, you just wanted to get straight down to business . . . To sum up, once night fell, you'd wander around the quayside, looking for couples, and when you saw one you'd crouch in the shadows and watch. After which, if a girl passed, you'd loom up in front of her, not quite sure what to say, looking like a madman, as one of them put it, and if she gave you time, you'd offer her money. If that didn't work, you'd go off and find the Marcotte woman . . . How old are you?'

'Twenty-five.'

'Aren't you ashamed to have such vices at your age?'

'I've always been alone . . .' Joseph stammered, as if talking to himself.

He didn't lower his eyes but looked the chief inspector full in the face, solemnly.

And to the surprise of both his mother and Hans, he went on, in that toneless voice he had begun to adopt:

'When I was small and occupied this same room, the house on the right hadn't been built yet. There was a patch of waste ground and, right up against the wall of our house, a grass embankment hidden, on the street side, by a stretch of fence. That was where couples came almost every night . . . There was a woman rather like Marcotte who'd go looking for bargees and bring them here. From my window, I'd watch . . .'

'Is that a reason to imitate them all your life?'

'I don't know. Maybe if people hadn't made fun of me . . . But I haven't done anything reprehensible.'

'On the evening of the 17th, you were at the fair, weren't you?'

'I dropped by.'

'You followed Sidonie and her friend.'

'I noticed them from a distance.'

'What did you do then?'

'Nothing. I went for a walk.'

Aunt Maria put her hand on Hans' arm and squeezed it.

'What time did you get home?'

'About eleven. I didn't check the time, but I'd definitely got back by eleven.'

'In that case, let me read you a statement by your neighbour Madame Guérin, the carpenter's wife . . .'

Aunt Maria stiffened and for a moment it looked as if she might open the door and rush into the next room to defend her son.

'". . . I had my neuralgia. I get it every two weeks or so. I'm sure of the date because it was the day my sister, who lives in Tilly, visited me. At half past ten, as I couldn't get to sleep, I took a pill and went and sat by the window. I went back to bed half an hour later. There's an alarm clock on the bedside table that lights up, so I could see what time it was. The pain was still there. At ten past eleven, I took another pill and went back to the window. From where I was, it was too dark to see the canal bank, and there wasn't any moon that night. The Krulls' cousin was the first to return home. He came along the street from the direction of town. It wasn't until well after midnight, when I was just about to go back to bed, that I saw Joseph Krull return home. He was coming from the direction of the canal . . ."'

A more troubling silence, Aunt Maria's hand tensing on Hans' arm.

'Do you still say you got back at eleven?'

'Yes.'

'Will you make a statement to that effect on oath?'

'Yes.'

Then immediately, in the same voice:

'No!'

The hand let go, and for a moment Aunt Maria left her listening post, because her legs had given out.

'I might as well tell you the truth. I followed Sidonie and her friend. Who knows, maybe I'd have tried again? At moments like these, you always hope—'

'That the fifty-franc note will do the trick!' the chief inspector cut in crudely.

'That the miracle will happen. That everything you've imagined while walking around for hours will come true.'

He wasn't ashamed, he was merely correcting the chief inspector. He knew these things better than the others, and he was telling it like it was.

'I think it happens to everyone. You see a woman pass in the street and you feel a sudden desire for her, you imagine that that desire can be realized, you conjure up every little detail—'

'Except that it doesn't happen to normal men with every woman who passes!'

'That's right,' he admitted. 'Perhaps because most men have other distractions. Not me.'

No, it was too difficult to explain! Especially as the two inspectors saw things differently from him, with all the exaggerated harshness of a police report.

'That evening, a man approached Sidonie.'

'What did he look like?' the man with the bad stomach asked ironically.

'I didn't see him very well. Quite tall, quite sturdy. Badly dressed, I think. I followed them . . .'

'Of course!'

'Why?'

'No reason. Go on.'

'I didn't immediately realize what was happening. I saw Sidonie struggling, but I didn't think it was serious. It was only afterwards . . .'

'How far away were you?'

'I don't know. Twenty metres maybe?'

'And you saw the man dragging the body to the canal?'

'Yes!'

'And you didn't intervene?'

'No!'

'And it didn't occur to you to inform the police? You just went calmly to bed?'

'Not calmly!'

'And the next day, you didn't tell anybody, not even your cousin?'

He shook his head. In all honesty, he had rarely been so calm. His body felt freer, as if it had been purged. Free and slightly empty, slightly floating . . .

'Do you realize the gravity of what you're saying?'

'I've told you the truth. I've never been a good liar.'

'Why didn't you inform the police?'

'Because the police hate us, like the whole neighbourhood, like my classmates at university, like everyone . . .'

The chief inspector glanced at his colleague, who shrugged.

'For any little thing, a minute's delay in closing the shop, they fine us.'

'Do you have anything else to add?'

'No, nothing.'

'Would you recognize the man who killed Sidonie?'

'I don't know.'

'And you haven't told anyone what you saw?'

Joseph hesitated. Aunt Maria, who had gone closer to the door, made a move as if she were going to prompt her son.

'No, no one.'

Then a much longer silence than the others. The two inspectors were standing by the window, conferring in low voices.

'We can't make any decision for the moment. It's up to the examining magistrate and he's in the country. In the meantime, we ask you not to go too far from this house. The house itself will be kept under surveillance.'

The door to the landing opened.

'Take us back to the lounge.'

Again, the three men's footsteps on the stairs. Hans and his aunt waited until they were below before they, too, went down. In the corridor, they ran into Joseph as he was coming out of the lounge.

'They're asking for you, Hans!' he said.

The inspector in the alpaca jacket was playing with the trinkets on the shelves, trinkets that were as banal as could be, the kind of objects you win in raffles, but which took on an exotic character in his podgy fingers.

The two men really were looking at the house as if they had never seen anything like it, as if everything – people and things – was questionable.

'Are you Hans Krull, from Emden?'

'Yes, inspector.'

'Give me your passport . . . Thank you! I'm taking it with me.'

'But—'

'You entered France without a visa, and I'm obliged to pass your papers on to the Sûreté. Until they make a decision, I forbid you to leave town.'

'All right, inspector.'

'Call Madame Krull.'

Having been listening behind the door, she came in immediately.

'As for you,' the chief inspector declared bad-temperedly, 'I advise you to be more cautious and to avoid incidents like the one this morning.'

'But, inspector, it was that woman who—'

'I'm asking you to avoid incidents. If the woman causes trouble when she's drunk, then simply refuse to serve her alcohol.'

Looking for the way out, he opened the wrong door and walked into the kitchen, where Anna had spread a dress pattern on the table and Liesbeth was sitting opposite, talking to her in a low voice.

The chief inspector looked as if he was thinking:

'Strange house!'

Joseph had gone back up to his room. The two men walked through the shop. Aunt Maria followed them, trying in vain to say something in mitigation.

The chief inspector paused for a moment by the zinc end of the counter and flicked at the tin spout on a bottle.

'If you don't want trouble, don't run a bar.'

As a result, when they had gone, Maria Krull looked at her own house with new eyes, searching for defects. Even the kitchen, for some reason, had offended the officers! Even the smell! Even the lounge!

She almost looked at herself in the mirror to figure out what it was about her that might explain their rude manner.

'What did they say?' Anna asked, pins between her lips.

'Nothing. Don't worry. Where's your father?'

'In the workshop.'

'Has he asked any questions?'

She took the opportunity to poke the stove. There were a lot of things to do, but not right away. The important thing was to calm down first. Joseph, upstairs, needed calm, too. As for

Hans, it was clear that he didn't need an immediate explanation either.

Suddenly, the house seemed cold, almost lifeless, as if a fearsome wind had swept through it. Every nook and cranny, every familiar object had become unrecognizable.

What was so special about it? Why did it arouse such aggressive feelings in people?

Before anything else, the normal atmosphere needed time to re-establish itself, the family members needed time to feel as if they were living their own lives again.

'Aren't you practising the piano, Liesbeth?'

Deliberately, she was saying it deliberately! At least if there was music, like the other days . . . But should they? Would people consider it an act of defiance or, on the contrary, a proof of innocence?

'Do you think so, Mother?'

Aunt Maria looked at Hans. Hans said:

'Oh, yes. Of course.'

It was especially urgent to keep busy, not to get under each other's feet, or look at each other with doom-laden eyes. Joseph had said what he had to say. Perhaps he had been right. They would have to wait to know what the consequences were.

And not look out at the quayside! Not bother with it!

'Would you like me to help you?' Maria Krull asked her daughter. 'Go and fetch my glasses. You're going to measure it all wrong again.'

The notes of the piano echoed as usual. Hans took the newspaper, planning to go out in the yard and read in the sun. But as he was putting his chair down by the door, Cornelius' assistant came to him and announced:

'The boss wants to see you.'

That gave him a shock. It was hard to imagine the silent Cornelius summoning someone to his workshop.

And yet that was the case! He was in his place, on his low chair with the sawn-off legs, a half-finished basket in front of him. The assistant resumed his place, too, as if it had been agreed since time immemorial that he was never in the way. And the fact that he was a hunchback, the fact that Uncle Cornelius looked like Saint Joseph, the silence of the workshop, the cool air, the sun-filled doorway gave the scene a strange solemnity.

'Hans, you have to leave here,' Uncle Cornelius said as the young man sat down on the chair he had adopted during his frequent visits.

'Leave? Why?'

'You have to leave.'

What happened now was that Hans, so brazen with everyone else, became, in the presence of this impassive old man, a little boy thrashing about awkwardly.

'Where can I go? If I return to Emden, what will I tell my father?'

Why did he instinctively sense that he was wrong to have said that? Without batting an eyelid, Cornelius slipped his hand into the pocket of his blue smock, took out an old postcard and handed it to his nephew. It was written in German and dated from fifteen years earlier. Below the text was stuck a cutting from an Emden newspaper about the tragic death of Peter Krull.

Cornelius didn't even look at his nephew to see what his reaction was. Only the assistant, like an archangel tasked with carrying out the Lord's wishes, had his eyes fixed on the young man.

Hans made an effort to smile.

'I'm so sorry. I confess everything. I didn't know where to go. I was being pursued because of my political opinions. I might have been sent to a concentration camp. Since you didn't know me, I told you about my father. I lied . . .'

'You have to leave,' the old man, still working, repeated with a stubbornness that made him even more similar to a Gothic saint.

'But Uncle Cornelius . . .'

For the first time in a long while, Hans was at a loss, and a little blood rushed to his cheeks. He saw now in his uncle something of his father, something indefinable, a kind of stubborn calm, a patient obstinacy which had led the other Krull to his over-complicated suicide.

When Hans was little, his father would say to him in the same tone:

'Eat your spinach!'

He never raised his voice. He didn't threaten, didn't lose his temper. He would repeat the sentence three times if necessary and he always ended up being obeyed.

Had anyone ever known what he thought? Did anyone know now what there was behind Cornelius' forehead the colour of yellowed ivory?

The card he had shown him was from Bisschoff the dollmaker, who lived in Emden right next to the Krulls' old house, the first one, the little cobbler's shop. So Cornelius had known for fifteen years!

And he hadn't said a word! He hadn't told anyone. He hadn't seen fit to inform his family, who didn't know his brother, that the man had killed himself.

He hadn't said anything to Hans when he had arrived . . .

What else did he know that he didn't say? What did he think about all day long, in his workshop, sitting beside his hunchbacked archangel?

What had he grasped of the drama that was being played out in the rest of the house, the drama of which everyone thought he was ignorant?

'You have to leave.'

'I can't leave immediately. The police have my passport.'

'You have to leave.'

'I don't have any money. Listen, uncle . . .'

Hans was clinging to the house. He didn't want to leave! He was panicking, looking for arguments, determined to sway this impassive man. He was losing all self-respect, deliberately forgetting that the hunchback could hear everything.

'If you throw me out, I'll be escorted to the German border. I'll go to prison. I didn't tell you, but I'm wanted by the police.'

It wasn't true. He was making up his arguments as he went along.

'You wouldn't like your brother's son to be sent to prison for theft. Listen, uncle—'

'You have to leave.'

'But when? I keep telling you, they won't let me go, the inspector took my passport . . . I lied to you, it's true. But what else did I do to you?'

'You have to!'

Other people's logic and pity as other people understood it were irrelevant. Cornelius had his own logic, a logic as mysterious as Hans' father's. And not only his logic! What kind of man was he to be able to live all his life in this workshop, even more removed from the world than a cloister, almost a stranger to his own family, who barely dared speak to him?

'I have something serious to confess, uncle. If you throw me out, you'll make Liesbeth very unhappy.'

There was no reply. Hans didn't care. He wanted to stay. It wasn't yet time for him to go. The drama wasn't over. He needed to be there to the end . . .

Like in Düsseldorf . . . It was one of the stories he had told. He had been staying with a female cousin who owned a perfume shop. She had a husband who worked for the railways and wore a dark-blue uniform. There was also a violinist who played in a local *Konditorei* and dropped in every day at the same time . . .

Hans loved the atmosphere of the shop, painted in pink and blue pastel tones. He revelled in the feminine atmosphere of the back room, where a bright-eyed manicurist operated.

Not that he had ever had his way with her. She was in love with a police constable who was often on duty at the corner of the street and with whom she went dancing on Sundays.

Hans was happy. He acted as a go-between for his cousin, an insipid blonde, and the violinist. He would carry notes from one to the other. He would stir both of them up. It was winter, with a lot of snow.

The violinist had come to visit several times, always in the afternoon, and Hans would smile, seeing him climb furtively to the apartment.

Then, one night, his cousin had woken with a start to find her husband cutting her hair. She hadn't understood. For a moment, she had thought he had gone mad, because he was usually a quiet man.

'Don't move!' he had ordered, pointing to a revolver on the bedside table.

He had cut off all her hair.

'The face your lover will make when he sees you like that! Now take off your nightdress . . . Take off your nightdress!'

He must have said it rather as Uncle Cornelius kept repeating:

'You have to leave!'

Then:

'Now go downstairs . . . Open the door . . . Open the door, I tell you! . . . Good! Now go to him . . . Go on, get out!'

He had thrown her out, stark naked, with a shaved head, on a December night.

Then he had come to Hans, who was sleeping on the floor above, in a former maid's room.

'Get up!'

He had given him two slaps, without anger, only contempt.

'Now get out of here!'

'Listen, uncle. Liesbeth and I love each other . . .'

Cornelius didn't react, continued weaving the immaculate wicker.

'If I leave, she'll be unhappy, her life will be ruined . . .'

He didn't care. He would go all the way. *He didn't want to leave the house!*

'I'm going to tell you everything. Liesbeth and I are lovers. We even . . .'

He would have sworn his uncle already knew. Did that mean he knew everything?

'Leave.'

'Today?'

'Leave.'

'At least give me until tomorrow. I have to go to the police station to demand my passport. You'll agree to that, won't you? Tomorrow, I promise . . .'

He was nothing but a boy, a little boy looking abashed. He had lost any prestige he had had.

'I promise you that tomorrow . . .' he repeated, not too sure what he was saying.

He stood up. He hadn't yet been able to meet the old man's eyes. He walked backwards to the door, giving the assistant a look full of hatred.

In the corridor, he shook himself, as if to break free of his stupor. Then, as he approached the door to the kitchen, he forced himself to whistle and only went in once he had completely resumed his nonchalant manner.

11.

Even though everyone was on the alert, even though they had been watching out for the slightest incident for some days now and had even been keeping an eye on one another, the event passed almost unnoticed. At any rate, nobody at the time anticipated the consequences.

The shop bell had rung. Maria Krull, who was in the kitchen, had glanced through the curtain, put the scissors down on the table and gone into the shop. Anna, who had been working with her, had glimpsed a customer, a bargee's wife with a child on her arm and others clinging to her skirts, and hadn't taken any notice.

'What do you want, Louise?' Maria Krull sighed, going behind the counter.

She was regaining the tone she had always had from before all these dramas, a sad, mournful tone. She seemed to be saying as she looked at her customer:

'You poor thing! In bad health again! And your kids not much better . . .'

Which was true. The woman she called Louise was the wife of the bargee from that morning, the man with the damp moustache and arrogant look who had flung his Pernod across the shop.

He gave her a child every year. There must be about ten of them still alive, and they all had the same hangdog look, the same stunned resignation.

As for the woman, she had one shoulder higher than the other, because of the youngest, whom she was perpetually carrying on her arm.

'Is it true he came in here and made a fuss?' she said first, because it was expected.

'You know how he is. He was already drunk.'

Aunt Maria knew most of the bargees and their families. Some had their post addressed to her house, and there was always a glass box full of letters hanging near the counter. She knew where they went and what they were carrying. She also knew when they would be paid.

'Give me five kilos of flour.'

Maria Krull didn't hesitate. She weighed the white flour in a large paper bag, then went to the drawer and took out the thick notebook with the elastic band in which she kept her accounts.

'I'd also like five kilos of beans and five kilos of split peas.'

Maria frowned. Nevertheless, she weighed the items and even, in accordance with custom, gave each of the children a sweet.

'Are you paying?'

'No! We'll be back next week to unload.'

With the purple pencil, Aunt Maria noted down the flour, the beans and the split peas at the bottom of a long column.

'I'll also have ten cans of sardines.'

That was what caused all the trouble. Maria Krull automatically did what she would have done any other day. She looked up in surprise and said quite curtly:

'I don't have any more, my girl!'

She was fine with extending credit to Louise for flour and starchy foods, but not for luxury commodities she didn't eat herself!

'I can see some there on the shelf.'

'Those are just for display.'

'You're only saying that because you don't want to serve me, aren't you?'

Louise wasn't spiteful, but she was stupid, and she was completely under her husband's thumb. Even now, she obeyed. She took a paper from her purse and said:

'I have a list he gave me: candles, starch, three cans of petrol, some—'

'Go and tell your man that if he wants provisions, he can start by paying me what he owes me.'

Louise stood motionless for a while in the middle of the shop, looking at Maria Krull as if waiting for something. Then she headed for the door, muttering:

'He'll beat me again!'

Through the window, Aunt Maria watched her drag herself across the central reservation. Muttering under her breath, she closed the notebook and put it back in the drawer.

A few moments later, Anna and her mother were again bent over the dress pattern. Liesbeth was still playing the piano. Hans was nowhere to be seen: he must have gone back up to his room.

Over by the barges, there was a group of men on the quayside, as usual when several boats were moored in close proximity. On board a big motor barge, they were taking advantage of the canal being shut down to do the washing.

Louise walked up to them with her children. Her husband, who was one of the group, yelled at her:

'Well? What about the provisions?'

'She wouldn't serve me.'

'What? She refused to serve you?'

'Listen . . .'

No, he wouldn't listen! He knew she was going to talk about money and he didn't want that. He turned to the others.

'Did you hear that? They're refusing to serve people now!'

Just then, Hans was at his window, so he could see the scene from a distance, but he attached no importance to it. It was the kind of scene you saw every day beside the canal: men in clogs, women on the boats, children playing like puppies near a pile of bricks, with the green of the trees all around them and the yellow tram ringing its bell in the foreground.

What surprised Hans more was seeing Monsieur Schoof and Marguerite coming along the street. He had forgotten that it was Thursday, their day. He hadn't realized that it was after six: on Thursdays, the Schoofs closed their shop at six to visit their friends the Krulls.

Anna was surprised, too. When the shop bell rang out and she glanced through the curtain, she said:

'Oh! It's already ten past six, and I haven't put my vegetables on yet!'

Soon afterwards, she called up the stairs:

'Joseph! Joseph! Marguerite's here!'

And from over there, from the canal bank, three angry-looking men, including Louise's husband, were starting in the direction of the Krull house.

At first, Louise hadn't admitted that the reason she had been refused service was because she owed more than three months' money. Nor had she said that the flour, the beans and the split peas had been weighed for her.

It was a bad day. The bargees were already in a foul mood because of the canal being shut down, which threatened to immobilize them for weeks. What had happened at the Tilly lock made it even worse, being something they had all been predicting for a long time.

Last but not least, they all owed larger or smaller sums of money to the Krulls, and each had his name in purple pencil in the notebook with the elastic band.

'She has no right to refuse to serve people . . .'

They were egging one another on, which helped to pass the time. The three men crossed the central reservation, beneath the trees, as Louise's husband had done by himself that morning, with the satisfaction of feeling everyone's eyes on them.

The policeman standing guard some thirty metres away saw them coming and moved closer, just in case. He was a pale young officer, face crushed beneath a cap that was too big for him.

He and the three men arrived in front of the shop at the same time. One of the men hailed the policeman:

'Hey, what do you think? Can shopkeepers refuse to serve a customer?'

Instead of replying, the policeman said:

'Just move on! We don't want any trouble.'

'I beg your pardon? You could answer me politely, for a start! The street belongs to everyone and, if I ask you for information, you're here to give it to me!'

'Don't shout so loud. Move on.'

Hadn't he been ordered to avoid a crowd forming in front of the house?

'We'll move on later. Right now we need provisions and, if they refuse to serve us, we want you to force them to—'

'Please, just move on.'

Passers-by stopped for a moment, thinking the men were drunks, which wasn't so far from the truth, as it happened. The other bargees, who had been following the scene from a distance, were approaching imperceptibly. Potut, dressed in the heavy overcoat he wore summer and winter, was lying asleep on a bench, his head on his folded arm.

'What's going on?' Monsieur Schoof asked in the kitchen, hearing noise.

'I don't know . . . More men who've been drinking . . .'

Hans was leaning out of his window.

'You still can't stop me from going into the shop!' Louise's husband declared. 'A shop is no different from the street. Provided you buy, everyone has a right to go in!'

And he tried to pass.

The policeman now made matters worse. He raised his whistle to his mouth and blew it to alert his colleague standing guard at the next crossroads.

At the shrill sound, which everyone recognized as a police whistle, onlookers appeared at the windows, and passers-by stopped to look.

The colleague, as regulations prescribed, set off at a run. And, seeing a uniformed officer running, people might well have assumed it was a serious event, a murder, a robbery or an arrest.

'Please just move on! If you don't, I warn you I'll take you to the station.'

'I'd like to see you try!'

'Well, you won't have long to wait.'

The other policeman arrived, out of breath.

'Can you take over here for a while, I'm taking this person to the station.'

'Who are you calling "this person"?'

'Just follow me or I'll fine you.'

The neighbour, Madame Guérin, was in her doorway. Louise was again crossing the central reservation, her child on her arm, two others still clinging to her skirts.

'Come with me, Désiré!' her husband said, as boastful as ever, to one of his companions. 'I'll tell that inspector . . .'

The new policeman didn't know anything and, as the three men moved away, he could only repeat without conviction:

'Move on, everyone! There's nothing to see.'

Anna had just laid the table and called out in the corridor:

'Dinner is served!'

And what surprised Monsieur Schoof the most, at that

moment, was seeing Hans come down and sit with the others. The little man writhed on his chair. He looked at each of them in turn, as if in search of an explanation. But Maria Krull was looking outside. Cornelius, in his wicker armchair, murmured:

'I think we should shut the shop.'

There was still nothing specific. They could see, from the back, the policeman's uniform. They were aware of groups of passers-by who had stopped to look. Most didn't even know what was happening. They asked:

'What's going on?'

And were told:

'I don't know . . .'

Or else:

'They refused to serve one of the bargees . . .'

Aunt Maria said with an anxious expression:

'Do you think we should lower the shutters?'

That struck her as a mistake. She couldn't explain why. In spite of herself she turned to Hans as if to ask his advice.

Then Cornelius, unusually for him, repeated without raising his voice, like a lament:

'I think we should shut the shop.'

She stood up, tightening her apron again. Hans stood up more quickly than her and said hurriedly:

'I'll do it, aunt.'

'But—'

He was already in the shop. The shutter over the window had to be closed from inside, by turning a handle. They heard its characteristic sound.

Monsieur Schoof took the opportunity to whisper in Maria Krull's ear:

'What are you going to do with him?'

He was talking about Hans. He couldn't understand why this young man who had lied and cheated him out of 5,000 francs was still there, sitting at the table with the others. It was even harder for him to understand Aunt Maria's reply:

'What *can* we do with him?'

He wasn't in the house from morning to night. He didn't know. He continued to feel ill at ease, looking at each of them in the hope of an explanation.

The noise of the shutter coming down at an unaccustomed time had somewhat the same effect as the policeman's whistle, causing the gathering outside to assume a more dramatic aspect. Nobody knew what it was all about, but it was obvious now that something was happening, and ten houses further on people were leaving their doorways to come and see.

They hadn't thought, in pulling down the shutter, that the word 'Kill!' could still be seen even though it had been painted over.

The glass door could be closed with the help of an outside shutter, but that had to be manoeuvred with a hook. Just as Hans was getting ready to do this, Maria Krull had a sudden reflex, perhaps an intuition, and called out:

'Hans!'

At that very moment, there was a crashing sound. A stone, thrown from the middle of the street, had hit the window bang in the middle of the advertisement for Reckitt's Laundry Blue.

Joseph leaped to his feet, very pale, stood there for a few seconds, his hands shaking, then sat down again, but nobody had even noticed. Cornelius, still bent over his plate, did not react. Monsieur Schoof stammered:

'What's got into them?'

A little boy's voice outside yelled:

'Thieves!'

The most extraordinary thing was that none of them left the table. It wasn't exactly deliberate, it was simply because nobody gave any signal to the contrary.

A second stone entered the shop and hit the door to the kitchen. Hans, meanwhile, got the shutter all the way down and hurriedly closed the door, so that all they could hear now was an indistinct murmur.

A tram passed with its usual clatter. In the kitchen, it was suddenly as dark as if it were dusk. Anna mechanically collected the plates.

It was then that Maria Krull was struck by Cornelius' attitude. He still hadn't moved. He was looking down at the tablecloth, and no emotion could be seen in his eyes. But he seemed older, all at once. There he was, silent, motionless, and nobody knew what he was thinking.

'Where are you going, Hans?'

'Upstairs. To have a look.'

They let him. When he was on the stairs, they were quite surprised to hear Cornelius say:

'I told him to leave.'

Joseph was deathly pale. His clammy hands were shaking. He was looking at all of them around the table with growing horror. He might have been the only one to know what the noises outside really meant.

'What's that?' Maria Krull said, giving a sudden start.

'The lounge . . .' Liesbeth stammered.

They hadn't thought about the two windows in the lounge, whose shutters were not closed. One of the windowpanes had just shattered. When Aunt Maria opened the door, she saw a half-brick on the table.

'Anna! Come and help me!'

It might have been expected that Joseph, as a man, would get up and help his mother. He had thought about it. He was making an effort and yet he stayed there, sweating, his Adam's apple going up and down.

'I'm coming, Mother.'

In the time it took them to bring down the two shutters, they saw almost nothing: figures, faces beyond the curtains, the policeman starting to lose his composure as he waited impatiently for his colleague to get back.

He didn't dare telephone for reinforcements. He was standing right up against the door, jammed against it, repeating stubbornly:

'Move on, there's nothing to see!'

How many people were there outside the house? Perhaps as many as thirty! The others, the neighbours, were keeping their distance further along the street.

Most of the crowd consisted of bargees, and some were no more aware of what was going on than the passers-by.

It was the hour when the workers came out of the Rideau boatyard. Passing on their bicycles, they stopped and asked bluntly:

'What are they doing to them?'

They lingered there, looking at the house front, their bicycles cluttering the roadway. Children ran between their legs. It was already impossible to say who had thrown the stones.

'I'd prefer it if the Schoofs left,' Maria Krull admitted to Anna while they were still in the lounge.

'We'll have to tell them . . .'

There were still five people at the table: Cornelius, Joseph, Monsieur Schoof, his daughter and Liesbeth. It was as if they didn't dare get up, as if they were afraid of what would happen when they abandoned their fixed poses.

Anna came back in. They didn't see Aunt Maria, who had gone upstairs. Hans was in Joseph's room on the first floor, standing at the window, behind the curtain.

She joined him and looked out, saw nothing but scattered groups who seemed to be waiting for something.

'What did Cornelius tell you?' she asked in a low voice.

'He said I should leave.'

Still looking outside but following her own thoughts, she said:

'You've done us so much harm!'

She turned abruptly.

'What are you doing here, Liesbeth?'

'But, Mother—'

'Go downstairs. Stay with your father.'

There were too many people in the house. Anna was right. They ought at least to get rid of the Schoofs, who had unwittingly wandered into something they didn't understand.

Monsieur Schoof was even saying to Cornelius:

'I always thought you were wrong to take that young man in.'

Cornelius didn't reply, of course, didn't even react. Marguerite was looking at Joseph with big eyes full of surprise and supplication.

And Aunt Maria said in a low voice to Hans, her hand shaking the curtain:

'I wonder what's going to happen . . .'

The people in the street had no idea about anything. Some were laughing. Others, having stayed a while, shrugged and left.

Nothing might have happened at all if someone hadn't gone to fetch Pipi from the bistro in Rue Saint-Léonard, where she had been drinking profusely.

They saw her coming from a distance, all worked up, her blouse open at the top. She knew she was the main protagonist and she elbowed her way into the middle of the crowd, where she planted herself, hands on her hips, raised her fist and cried:

'So, is it true they're going to be arrested? The thieves! The murderers!'

A well-dressed gentleman in a bowler hat, who took her for just any old drunk, must have told her to be quiet because he was the one she took it out on. She needed a sparring partner and she had found him. She screamed:

'What did you say? Don't make a scene? You're one to talk! Did these people kill your daughter? No? Then shut up!'

There was again some laughter, a few smiles, but not as many as before. People came closer to get a better look, to hear what was being said.

'There! It was there, just opposite their house! They should never have let these Germans into the country . . . And that Joseph of theirs, the big lout who followed all the local girls . . . When I think that his mother offered me money to keep me quiet!'

And, looking around her defiantly:

'That's right! She offered me money. Ask her if you don't believe me! I even went and told the inspector . . .'

Hans looked at his aunt. She was pale. She didn't protest.

It was true that she had begged Pipi to stop accusing them. She had reminded her of the baby clothes she had given her, the credit she had extended to her, the New Year gifts . . .

In the end she had stammered:

'You know I'm good, you know I'll never leave you in the lurch.'

Which was precisely what Pipi was now saying, out there in the street:

'She told me how good she was, how she would never leave me in the lurch.'

The policeman, trapped near the door, didn't dare intervene but kept looking along the street, waiting for his colleague to return. Even when he at last saw him coming with a sergeant, he merely ventured:

'Move on! Come on now, move on!'

Nobody was paying any attention to him. A mother said to her little girl, because of Pipi's crude language:

'Go and play! This is no place for children.'

Determined to assert his authority as soon as he arrived, the sergeant tore into the crowd.

'Have you people quite finished? . . . Pipi, if you don't shut up, I'll take you to the cells . . . Come on now! I don't want to see anybody out in the street from now on.'

The crowd visibly retreated, but only for a few seconds, because immediately afterwards they pushed forwards again, voices raised in protest, especially after the sergeant grabbed Pipi's arm.

'Let go of me!' she yelled. 'You're hurting me! Let go of me, you filthy brute!'

'Leave her alone!' cried a bargee who was half a head taller than everybody else.

'Shut up, you!'

'What? Did you just tell me to shut up? Want to repeat that?'

'I don't know what they've got over the police!' Pipi cried. 'It's obvious they're protecting them! I guess you have to be German!'

Upstairs, Hans asked:

'Where's Joseph?'

'In the kitchen.'

'What's he saying?'

'Nothing . . .'

It was true. He had now taken refuge in the lounge, and Marguerite, tactless and stubborn, had followed him.

'What do they want?' she asked him. 'I don't understand what's got into them.'

He was in such a panic that he couldn't answer. He would have liked to react. Earlier, he had made up his mind that he, not Hans, would close the shutters, but he had been unable to move.

He was scared! It was physical. The whole of his big body had broken out in a cold sweat, and at times he was on the verge of throwing up, there and then, even though Marguerite was present.

Liesbeth wasn't in the kitchen. Nobody knew where she was. Only the two old men were left, Cornelius still motionless, Monsieur Schoof anxious. Anna, perhaps unthinkingly, served them coffee, just as she did every Thursday.

'Would you like the light on?' she asked.

Her father didn't reply. Monsieur Schoof said:

'There's no need.'

The sergeant was no longer as cocksure as before, and regretted that he hadn't brought other men with him. He whispered to one of the two officers:

'Go and phone the inspector.'

'Is he at the station?'

'No, he's at home! Tell him . . . Tell him he has to come . . .'

He had a sense that something bad was going to happen, even though there was as yet nothing specific. It was like a sky that turns leaden, the sun too heavy and too hot, until eventually the storm clouds gather.

The trams were still passing. Neighbours in the doorways were chatting without suspecting that things might take a tragic turn, and there was still laughter, people calling to each other.

'Hey, Marcel! Shall we go and have dinner?'

Or else, in a high-pitched voice:

'Émile! Émile! Your mother's calling you!'

But people didn't retreat when the uniformed officers advanced towards them. Some now had a harder expression on their faces. Pipi, feeling supported, raised her fists, attaining a degree of pathos in her drunken state.

'He'd been following her for weeeks,' she said, genuinely in tears. 'The poor girl didn't want anything to do with him, even if he was a doctor. He offered her money . . . In that house, all that matters is money . . . When he saw there was nothing doing, he attacked her by the canal and strangled her.'

A woman dabbed at her eyes. Pipi looked at her audience, spotted a red hat near the back row and called out:

'Come here, Germaine! Tell them what you know. Tell them about that evening when he kept following the two of you.'

She hadn't prepared any of this. Drunkenness gave Pipi the instincts of an actress. She stooped and clasped the girl with the big breasts and big buttocks in her arms. This started the girl crying, too.

'Come on now, calm down, both of you,' the sergeant said in a conciliatory tone.

But the others now turned against him.

'Shut up!' someone cried.

'Down with the cops!' someone else cried from the back row.

Without being aware of it, Monsieur Schoof had lit his meerschaum pipe and stretched his short legs as he usually did. He repeated with gentle stubbornness:

'I don't understand how you could have kept that young man.'

Nervously, Joseph cracked his fingers as he pulled on them and implored Marguerite:

'Leave me alone.'

'No, Joseph! If you're upset, I'm the one you should tell.'

Even though she could hear voices from outside, she didn't understand!

'What are they saying?' she asked. 'Who are they angry with?'

Upstairs, Aunt Maria and Hans were still standing side by side, stock still, ears pricked . . .

'What are they waiting for? Why don't they arrest them?'

'Who?' asked someone who had just arrived.

'The murderer!'

'What murderer?'

'Sidonie's murderer!'

Hearing her daughter's name, Pipi involuntarily burst into tears and threw herself on the ground in a fit of despair.

'My little girl . . . My little girl . . .' she stammered. 'Someone give her back to me! Someone give me back my little girl, my angel . . .'

Some of the onlookers were sniffling. Most of them didn't know the woman was drunk.

'Get up . . .' the sergeant begged her. 'Please get up . . .'

But he was given such angry looks that he didn't dare insist.

The young policeman came back from telephoning and announced:

'He's on his way!'

Beyond the dark-green foliage of the trees, the sky was beginning to darken, turning red before attaining the purple of a summer evening.

The locals who at this hour were in the habit of strolling by the canal for a little fresh air approached timidly, especially those who had children and who formed small groups some thirty or forty metres away.

'Come here, Jojo! I forbid you . . .'

There were loving couples.

'Let's go,' he would say.

And she would reply:

'Just another minute . . .'

To see if something was finally going to happen!

'Who are they?'

'Germans . . .'

'What have they done?'

'Apparently they killed a girl . . .'

The most telling thing was what the carpenter next door did. Presumably thinking that his own house was as exposed as the Krulls', he, too, closed his shutters.

The people in the back rows were joking. Some were only

there because others were and they got up on tiptoe, apologizing to those they jostled.

Others, around Pipi, were starting to mutter angrily, especially when Louise's husband, who had been released, came and planted himself in front of the sergeant.

'Going to arrest me again, are you? Are you working for the Germans, too?'

Those were the words that recurred most frequently: 'the Germans!' Some people, on arriving, heard only those syllables.

And now, for no specific reason, the crowd pressed forwards, perhaps simply because someone had lost balance.

'Move back! Move back!' cried the sergeant, holding the two officers by the hand to form a barrier.

'Move back yourself!' retorted the huge bargee.

The policemen, pushed back by the crowd, thudded against the shutters, and under the impact the last shards came loose from the broken windowpanes, releasing a shower of glass into the shop.

'I think we'd better go!' Monsieur Schoof said, getting to his feet.

To which Cornelius responded, like an echo:

'I think so.'

The kitchen was in semi-darkness now. Anna wiped her eyes. Her father, still motionless, seemed to fade gradually into the gloom.

12.

There were absurd little touches. For example, when Maria Krull returned, preoccupied, to the kitchen and saw Monsieur Schoof getting to his feet, her face automatically took on another expression, the expression of a hostess, and she said in polite surprise:

'Leaving already?'

It was only a reflex, and immediately afterwards she was back to the way she had been before, the way the others were, looking around her, brow furrowed with the effort of focusing her mind, anxious to know what was going on.

'Has Marguerite gone?'

Because the most curious thing was how lost they were.

All the doors were open, like lock gates, between the different parts of the house. The air was circulating freely. They passed without seeing each other. A moment earlier, Anna had been in the kitchen and now she wasn't. And where was Joseph? Everyone was drifting in and out, apart from the two old men rooted in the kitchen.

But now Monsieur Schoof was on his feet, looking for his hat and calling:

'Marguerite!'

She was coming! She was in the lounge, standing by Joseph, who kept clenching his teeth with impatience. For the last five minutes, gently, stupidly, she had been trying to worm information out of him.

'What did he do? Why won't anyone tell me?'

Because she put everything that was happening down to Hans! She had never been so pink, an improbable pink so reminiscent of a cow's udders that you expected to see her giving milk!

'I'm coming, Daddy . . . Good night, Joseph. Promise me you'll keep calm.'

She gave him her slightly blotchy cheeks to kiss, then rushed out of the lounge with feigned breeziness.

'Where's Liesbeth? Liesbeth! Come and say goodbye to Monsieur Schoof.'

Had everybody taken their leave? In the end, the pace quickened. Monsieur Schoof moved towards the door. Aunt Maria was already turning the key and listening.

'Be quick,' she said in a low voice.

They squeezed through. Their appearance in the doorway was greeted with a whistle from a boy of fifteen in one of the last rows, who had stuck four fingers in his mouth. The shrill sound had the same effect as the policeman's whistle. It caused a riot. Immediately, other whistles rang out. One whole section of the crowd took it up, for fun, just to hear themselves, while Monsieur Schoof, holding Marguerite by the hand, slipped past the houses.

Some people, who had only stayed out of idleness, thought it was over, especially as some failed attempts at whistling provoked bursts of laughter. But that was in the back rows. In the front rows, people were pressing around Pipi, who was recounting her misfortunes, and even those who knew her ended up feeling sorry for her this evening.

Somewhere near the tram rails, the wife of a bargee was explaining to people who weren't from the canal:

'They even charge us five centimes more for sugar! Those people take advantage of the fact that we can't always pay cash.'

It was true. All the merchandise in the Krulls' shop was a

little more expensive than anywhere else. But how many accounts recorded in the big black notebook were still unpaid?

'Once, they lent money to the master of the *Belle Hélène* and, when he couldn't pay it back, they got the bailiffs in.'

Nobody paid any attention to who was leaving and who was coming. In fact, most of those leaving were respectable middle-class people from the surrounding area, who had seen something in passing or while taking their evening constitutional.

In their place, young men appeared, especially young men in caps who deliberately acted tough and looked around them insolently.

One of these thought he spotted a silhouette behind a curtain on the first floor.

'There! Aim at the brother!'

He picked up a brick, threw it and hit the window full on. Hans just had time to move out of the way.

This was a signal. The pile of bricks was quite close. Other hooligans went to fetch them and flung them haphazardly at the upper floor. Many of the bricks fell back on to the pavement, and people had to move out of the way.

A tram rang its bell in vain for two minutes as it tried to make its way through the crowd, which, as if by magic, had become more dense. The policemen had red brick dust on their tunics.

And the whistles started up again, even more forcefully than before, when they saw four policemen arrive on bicycles, followed by the inspector, who was still wearing his boater.

'Kill the Kraut!' they cried. 'Kill the murderer!'

It was exciting to throw bricks at that façade, behind which nothing could be seen. Some fell into the rooms on the first floor.

A voice said:

'Who knows? They're quite capable of shooting at us!'

Others heard only the last words:

'Careful, they're going to shoot at us!'

They thought they glimpsed shadowy figures behind the broken windows. For a long time they took as a target a curtain quivering in the breeze, behind which they assumed there was an enemy.

Mopping his brow, the inspector got up on the doorstep and tried to obtain silence in order to speak to the crowd. A fragment of brick knocked his straw hat off, which provoked a mixture of laughter and jeers.

As in a fire, the excitement would diminish in one sector, die down completely, only to flare up somewhere else.

Beyond the roadway, the central reservation was deserted apart from a man sitting on a bench. It was Potut, wrapped in his thick overcoat, his hands in his pockets, an unlit pipe planted in his beard. He was watching, placid and indifferent.

And now people were arriving in groups, in gangs, from the working-class neighbourhoods. These, as soon as they arrived, were bolder and more aggressive.

'Down with the cops!'

The neighbours, stunned by what had happened, realized that things were becoming serious. They kept a cautious distance. They had put their children to bed, and from time to time they would move closer, casting worried glances, wondering where it was all going to end.

'It's their fault, too! They've always refused to be like everyone else!'

From a nearby house, the inspector was phoning in vain to the prosecutor, the examining magistrate, the town hall. Everyone was in the country!

He next turned to the gendarmerie and called it to the rescue.

'Yes . . . Send men . . . As many as you can . . . Until then, I can't be held responsible.'

Bad-tempered voices were crying:

'What are they waiting for? Why don't they arrest him?'

Cornelius was still sitting alone in his armchair in the now completely dark kitchen. Occasionally someone would come in and go out again, barely recognizable from the rustle of a dress, the sound of footsteps.

Joseph was still in the lounge. Protected by the shutters, he was listening, pale-faced, wild-eyed.

Two or three times, his mother had joined him and put her hand on his shoulder.

'They won't dare . . . The police are there . . .'

But he was barely capable of answering her. He looked at her as if he didn't recognize her, or didn't hear her. He was shaking. His whole body was in a state of panic, his nerves had given way abruptly.

'It's late. People will go to sleep in the end.'

Why did Joseph think the crowd was going to set fire to the house? It was a vision he had had. He had imagined flames passing in front of his eyes, had seen himself running in all directions in the inferno and finding no way out.

'Keep calm.'

Where was she going? Why were people constantly going up and down the stairs? And when they passed, they pretended not to see each other!

The bricks were hitting the front of the house at a less rapid pace now, but the people outside had already moved on to something else. Dozens of voices were chanting in unison, as if under the direction of an orchestra conductor:

'The-mur-der-er! . . . The-mur-der-er! . . . The-mur-der-er! . . .'

'Gentlemen!' the inspector made an effort to yell, standing on tiptoe.

'The-mur-der-er!'

'Gentlemen!'

He received something dirty full in the face: a cloth, a soft, damp object that must have been picked up from the gutter.

'The-mur-der-er! . . . The-mur-der-er!'

The chorus was growing louder, the rhythm more pronounced.

'I have to talk to them from the window,' the inspector said to his sergeant.

Crossing the pavement, which was strewn with bricks, he knocked at the door.

That was another mistake. The voices became more urgent.

'In the name of the law . . .'

'Mother!' Anna, who was in the shop, called out.

She thought her mother was far away, perhaps upstairs, and now she heard her skirt, quite close by. Bending by the door, Maria Krull asked:

'Who is it?'

'The inspector.'

The others were still yelling.

'Listen, inspector,' she said in a measured tone. 'If I open the door, the crowd will come in. You should go through the house next door.'

He had presumably understood, because they didn't hear any more from him. But they did hear jeering, as well as more whistling. The noise was turning nastier.

It was because the gendarmes had just arrived and were advancing threateningly. There was jostling, and blows were exchanged in the front rows. The people in the other rows were pushed back several metres and found themselves jammed up against the trams, of which there was already quite a queue.

Occasionally, like a rocket going higher in a firework display, there came an isolated cry:

'Kill him!'

Meanwhile, Maria Krull stopped by her husband's armchair and said in a low voice:

'You should go to bed, Father!'

Only his face and beard could be seen. He nodded and said:
'I will.'

But he didn't move.

Liesbeth was on her knees in her parents' bedroom, praying to a large ebony crucifix.

Hans was wandering about. Nobody now seemed to hear him or even suspect his existence. It was he, looking out of a window on the landing, who was the first to see the inspector in the neighbouring garden. The carpenter, who was also there, placed a ladder against the wall, and the inspector climbed it and called out:

'Is there anyone in there!'

Hans made to go. In the corridor, he bumped into his aunt, who ordered:

'Leave it.'

A moment later, the inspector came into the house, right in front of Aunt Maria, and looked around him with even more suspicion than during the afternoon, as if afraid of the slightest patch of shadow.

'Where is he?'

'In the lounge.'

'I think it's best if I arrest him provisionally. I haven't found anyone to give me instructions. If I leave him here, the crowd will end up forcing the doors.'

He didn't feel sorry for them. Right now, he shared the crowd's hostility towards the Krulls and its disgust for Joseph.

Outside, a gendarme who didn't know the situation had manhandled Pipi, and that had provoked renewed anger.

'I'm going upstairs to talk to them.'

Maria Krull went up behind him, her steps so muffled that she seemed like his shadow. Passing an open door, they saw Liesbeth on her knees, then brushed against Anna, who was standing against a doorpost.

'I think I should put my scarf on. Fortunately, I always have it on me.'

He groped his way in the semi-darkness, took a deep breath and rushed to the window, where he emerged like a puppet, making feverish gestures with his too short arms.

'Gentlemen! Gentlemen! I demand silence!'

But all he obtained was laughter, followed by a shower of missiles, some of which even ended up on the landing.

'I'm about to arrest Joseph Krull! I ask you to remain calm!'

He didn't know what to say, terrified by the magnitude of the spectacle in front of his eyes, the long line of yellow trams trapped in the crowd, all those faces raised towards him.

'Once Joseph Krull has been arrested, you can all go home.'

Surprisingly, there was a moment of silence, of hesitation, and he took advantage of it to withdraw. But he hadn't reached the foot of the stairs, still followed by Maria Krull, when the cry again went up:

'Kill him! Kill him!'

He no longer knew what to do, lost control of his nerves and caught himself saying:

'This is all your fault! Where is he?'

Joseph was there, standing in front of him.

'I'm arresting you without arresting you. The reason I'm taking you to prison, even though I don't have a warrant, is because it's the only way to pacify the crowd.'

Joseph said nothing. His Adam's apple was moving. His fingers were almost tangled. Mechanically, he followed the inspector into the shop, but there, by the door, which was again being shoved from outside, he was able finally to whisper:

'They're going to kill me . . .'

He was scared. He couldn't help it: his teeth were chattering! His whole body was afraid, his whole body was giving way, and he looked as if he might faint at any moment.

'You'll have to take him through the neighbours' house,' a voice said. 'At the bottom of their garden, there's a door that leads to the street behind.'

It was Hans speaking. They all looked at each other, still in the semi-darkness. They were waiting for the inspector to make up his mind. He finally declared:

'It's worth a try . . .'

Aunt Maria threw herself into her son's arms, but there was no reaction from his big body.

'Be brave!' she said.

Liesbeth did not come down. Anna, like her mother, said:

'Be brave, Joseph!'

He let himself be taken out, moving as he had when he was a sleepwalker. They had forgotten all about Cornelius. The old man, huddled deep in his armchair, did not get up, just watched the strange procession as it brushed past him.

Anyone could have climbed over the separation wall, and yet so clumsy was Joseph that they had to give him a push and hold him up. There were people at the windows, pointing him out to each other. But the neighbours didn't raise the alarm, preferring to keep out of it.

Aunt Maria quickly came back into the kitchen, wiping her eyes.

'You should go to bed, Father! Come . . .'

Helping Cornelius to his feet, she said softly:

'It's better this way. They'll release him tomorrow. At least he's safe . . .'

He went up by himself. Liesbeth, seeing him come in, left the room. There were still as many cries, still as much stir outside, but it all seemed less serious now that Joseph had gone.

Besides, the carpenter now came out of his house, looking self-important, and cautiously approached the groups.

'They've taken him away,' he announced.

'Who?'

'The murderer! He even came through my house! The inspector took him out the back way.'

'Who went out the back way?' cried a bad-tempered voice.

'The murderer!'

'Has he run away?'

Two different rumours were circulating: the first was that Joseph Krull had run away (it was even said that he had broken his leg jumping through a window), but then the better-informed asserted that he had been taken to prison.

Maria Krull was as weary as if she had done a fortnight's wash all by herself. And yet she was still standing! It was as if she was afraid to sit down.

She went into the lounge, started up the stairs, opened the door to her room and heard a voice saying to her:

'Hans will have to go . . .'

Old Cornelius could not be seen because the room, the least exposed in the house, was now in complete darkness. That was perhaps why these words had a particular resonance, taking on the weight of an utterance by a biblical prophet.

'Try to sleep, Father!'

Ever since they had had children, she had always called him that.

'He'll have to go!' he repeated.

'Yes . . . Tomorrow . . .'

She closed the door again, went into the next room, her son's room, and realized that the agitation had not yet receded.

She glided across the polished wooden floor and went downstairs. She hesitated to switch the lights on, for fear that the slightest glimmer would excite those outside even more.

'Are you here, Anna?'

'Yes, Mother.'

'What about Liesbeth?'

'I don't know where she is. In the lounge, perhaps?'

Maria Krull went there, to avoid leaving her daughter with Hans. But he wasn't in the lounge. From time to time, they saw him pass, looking helpless, searching for his place, feeling that the walls themselves were rejecting him.

'Come, Liesbeth. You're going to drink something before going to bed.'

The inspector was back outside the house. He was moving about a lot, gesticulating, shouting, charging into the groups.

'I tell you I've just had him taken to prison! Ask the carpenter next door. So there's nothing more for any of you to do here.'

As for the girl in the red hat, her mother had long since fetched her and taken her home. The girl had thrown a tantrum in her bed because she hadn't been allowed to see everything through to the end.

'If you don't disperse, I'll call the fire brigade, and they'll turn their hoses on you.'

There was still some anger, but also a lot of laughter. The driver of the first tram in the line wisely decided to ring his bell insistently and move forwards in slow motion, pushing part of the crowd back towards the central reservation.

'He's been arrested!' the policemen yelled, cupping their hands. 'Go home, or the firemen will turn their hoses on you!'

Maria Krull made up her mind to turn the light on in the kitchen, poked the stove mechanically and shook the coffee pot, in which there was still some lukewarm coffee left.

'Fetch the rum, Anna.'

In normal circumstances, they had to be ill to be allowed alcohol. But Aunt Maria herself poured some into her daughter's coffee, and an unaccustomed smell of hot rum hovered in the kitchen.

Nobody was paying any attention to Hans. He stood there with his back to the door frame. They didn't offer him coffee.

'It seems to be quietening down,' Anna said.

'It's almost midnight!'

It was rare, in this house, to see the pale clock face mark such an hour! But they were so exhausted, their nerves so shaken, that nobody made a move.

They weren't thinking. They were listening to the noises from outside, which they could no longer distinguish one from another. The bells of the trams were already like a promise of a return to life.

Putting on a bold front, Hans lit a cigarette and remained to the end. The three women were finally sitting, their elbows on the table.

'It isn't a real arrest,' Aunt Maria said, as if to answer certain unspoken questions.

Because Joseph was in prison!

'As long as he doesn't panic,' Anna said.

They all retained a painful image of Joseph. They would have liked to buck him up, put him back on his feet.

Anna, going from one thought to another, said:

'I kept wondering when the Schoofs would finally decide to leave . . . Marguerite didn't understand a thing . . .'

For hours now Liesbeth had wanted to cry, but she was so tense that she couldn't.

Outside, the moon was up, and the various groups exchanging noisy comments as they made their way home were reminiscent of those evenings when a fireworks display brings an unexpectedly large number to the same spot.

The gendarmerie remained outside the house, along with the police. Some groups lingered, but they were mostly young men having fun, making loud jokes.

The mood in the kitchen was heavy. The light itself was heavier than on other evenings. When someone knocked at the door of the shop, everybody gave a start. Maria Krull got to her feet.

'Who is it?'

'The inspector. You can open the door now.'

Once the door was finally open and the moonlight streamed in, a strange spectacle presented itself: the shop in chaos, shards of glass strewn over the floor.

'I've come to tell you it's over. As you can see, it was the only way to calm them down. All the same, I'm leaving some men on guard all night.'

He would have liked to see what was going on inside the house. The light in the kitchen intrigued him. He tried to see over Maria Krull's shoulder, but she simply said as she closed the door:

'Thank you.'

She pulled the bolts and came back to the kitchen.

'We should sleep,' she said.

Nobody was sleepy, but they had to pretend to sleep! They had to get up, climb the stairs, say goodnight just like any other day, because in spite of everything life continued.

Hans still didn't count. They avoided acknowledging that he was there, especially Liesbeth, who hadn't once looked his way.

'Goodnight, Anna!'

'Goodnight, Mother.'

'Goodnight, Liesbeth!'

They reached the first floor. Maria Krull opened the door to her bedroom and noiselessly switched on the light.

'Where's your father?'

The others stopped and saw the empty bed, the still undisturbed sheets.

'Anna! Liesbeth! Your father!'

Aunt Maria ran down the stairs and rushed first to the lounge. Liesbeth called:

'Father! Father!'

It seemed to all of them as if a draught had blown past them, as if there was a new emptiness in the house. They switched the lights on as they advanced, including those in the shop, and the light inevitably brought out the chaos and damage.

'It isn't possible!'

As Aunt Maria, in desperation, approached the workshop, she saw Hans opening the door. He had gone there instinctively! He left it to his aunt to switch on the light.

There was a muffled sound, the sound of Maria Krull falling to her knees, then a piercing cry from Liesbeth.

'What's going on?' Anna asked, wild-eyed.

The workshop was the only room that hadn't been touched by the chaos. The naked bulb crudely illumined the whitewashed walls, the half-finished baskets, the chairs where Cornelius and his assistant always sat.

Right beside Cornelius' chair, a shadowy figure was swinging, casting an even longer shadow on the wall.

'Father! Father!'

They hadn't seen him come downstairs. They didn't know when he had left his room. But then it had always been his custom to move noiselessly about the house.

And to say nothing.

He had hanged himself, nobody knew exactly why. But did they know why, after his wanderings, he had settled on the edge of this town, why, for years, he had lived silently in this workshop with his hunchbacked assistant?

What did they know about him?

He had come here alone. He had remained alone amid his family, with his patriarch's beard and his mysterious or serene face. And he had left alone. He had hanged himself in his corner, near his chair with the sawn-off legs and a white wicker basket that would never be finished.

He had said nothing, and it was somewhat alarming, now, to wonder what he knew.

It was tempting to think that he had come not simply from Emden, an artisan wandering through Germany and France, but from much further away in space and time, from a fixed world depicted in Bible images, in church sculptures, in stained-glass windows.

'No!' Aunt Maria simply said as Hans stepped forward to take him down.

Liesbeth threw herself on the floor in a fit of hysterics, her cries reminiscent of those heard earlier in the street.

'Shhh, be quiet!' Anna said to her mechanically, her nerves equally on edge.

Hans retreated. In this room with its overly white walls, its one light bulb, they were all unwittingly making the shadows dance.

Aunt Maria had climbed on to the low chair.

'Pass me a knife, Anna,' she said, articulating the words clearly.

Liesbeth's sobs must have been tearing her chest apart.

'Where is it, Mother?'

'There must be one on the workbench.'

Words that needed to be said, but which sounded hollow!

'Careful. Hold him.'

Hans was glued to the wall as if afraid, both hands flat on the whitewashed bricks.

'Don't drop him.'

God alone knew how they managed it. The body descended slowly, and the head tilted and came to rest on the unfinished basket, which formed a pillow.

Maria Krull hadn't yet cried. The stiff lines of her bodice, the folds of her black dress made her look like a statue.

Especially when she walked over to Hans and said to him:

'You have to leave.'

'But—'

'You have to leave, Hans. Now!'

He caught fright. He looked at the three of them. Perhaps he felt that it was his turn to be the Foreigner, the cause of all the ills in the world?

'Monsieur Schoof's money . . .' he began, moving his hand to his pocket.

'Just go!'

'Liesbeth!'

She didn't respond to him, didn't turn her head.

He ran to the shop, pulled back the bolts, opened the door and almost bumped into two policemen on guard duty and some gendarmes telling each other stories.

'What is it?' they asked him.

'Nothing! I'm going out . . .'

As long as he was within their field of vision, he had to force himself to walk at a normal pace.

Were people a little ashamed in the morning? Perhaps. But they were curious, too. They watched from a distance, the neighbours pretending to be drawn outside by some occupation or other.

At 8.30, they saw Madame Krull already coming back from town, where she had gone very early. She was wearing her black dress and her hat with the strings. The policemen moved aside for her.

She simply went into the house and came back out, without having taken off her hat, but bringing a chair and a hammer.

And on the shutter, which echoed now as it had echoed the day before to the impact of the bricks, she nailed a white sign with a black border, which she had gone to buy from a printer:

Closed due to bereavement

13.

It was years later, in Stresa, in the middle of August, when the heat was at its height. Waiting for the daily storm to break, which would only happen at the end of the day, Lake Maggiore was like a cauldron, the water so thick-looking it was as if the boats were caught in it, unable to get free.

On the promenade, the asphalt was melting. The hundreds of windows on the white façades of the big hotels were dark holes, like the cells of honeycombs.

Near the landing stage, where two travel agencies competed by means of gaudy posters and loudspeakers, coaches stopped, blue ones, yellow ones, black ones, filled to capacity, covered in dust, coming from Switzerland, Belgium or France, disgorging identical crowds in light-coloured suits and white dresses, dazed and exhausted from too many stops, too many arrivals and departures, too many hastily eaten meals, dragging with them children, coats, cameras and suitcases and only daring to look up at the Italian sky through dark glasses.

'Joseph! Hold the boy!'

Three coaches had arrived simultaneously, but the passengers were not all scheduled to have lunch at the same hotel, and everyone was lost. There were loudspeaker announcements:

'Passengers on the blue coach! Passengers on the blue coach! Lunch will be at the Hôtel des Grottes. Departure at exactly 1.45.'

'Passengers from Geneva! Passengers from Geneva! Lunch at the Hôtel du Lac. Departure at . . .'

People searched for and lost each other, some asking information of a postcard seller.

Joseph was wearing a grey suit, a Panama hat and an open-necked shirt and holding a thin, fair-haired, spindly-legged seven-year-old boy by the hand.

'Look, Daddy—'

'Joseph! Tell Anna off! She doesn't want to walk.'

The girl was three years old, as round and pink as her mother.

'Anna, if you refuse to walk . . .'

People who had been here for weeks passed by, looking ironically at those pouring off the coaches. A couple stopped. A man called:

'Joseph!'

It was so sunny and the air so sparkling that it was hard to see, and even the sounds became blurred.

'Did somebody just call you?' Marguerite asked.

'I don't know.'

They looked around them and spotted a middle-aged woman with a painted face. Her nails were painted, too, even her toenails, which protruded from curious-looking sandals.

She wasn't the one who had called. She was as surprised as they were. Her companion had left her suddenly and run forwards.

It was Hans, in white trousers, also barefoot in sandals, his skin tanned.

'Joseph! What a nice surprise!'

The children, the boy especially, were looking at him in terror.

'Let me introduce Lady Bramson, a good friend of mine . . . My cousin Joseph and his wife . . . Well, Joseph?'

'Well, nothing!' he replied, coldly.

'Did everything work out? Just imagine, I had to go abroad right away. I did look in the newspapers, but there was nothing . . .'

Marguerite, who had recognized Hans, was pulling her husband's arm, the little boy the other arm.

'Still up there?'

'Yes.'

'And Aunt Maria?'

'She's there, too.'

'What about the shop?'

Joseph nodded involuntarily, all the while looking for a way to escape.

'What about Anna?'

'She's with her.'

'And Liesbeth?'

'She's married . . . If you don't mind, our coach—'

'Are you touring Italy?'

Joseph had grown a little ginger moustache that made his face look different.

Lady Bramson was getting impatient. She had a fox terrier on a lead, and it was pulling away.

'Are you a doctor?'

'Yes.'

'In the house that . . .'

Fortunately the guide from the French coach spotted Joseph and cried through his loudspeaker:

'Passengers from the blue coach are asked to sit down to lunch. We leave again in twenty minutes.'

Hans was still trying to talk. 'I'm here with a friend who . . .'

A handshake.

'Yes . . . Goodbye . . .'

'Goodbye. Did . . .'

Already the Krulls were swallowed up by the crowd on the terrace, where lunch was being served at breakneck speed.

'Who was that?' Hans' companion asked.

'A strange character. It's quite a story.'

He grabbed the fox terrier's lead and took a few steps in silence. His companion took out a gold lighter and lit a cigarette.

'It was bound to end like that!'

'What was bound to end like that?' she asked, not attaching any great importance to the subject.

To which he replied, in the same tone:

'Nothing . . . Joseph . . . The whole thing . . .'

They went to get the English papers from the news vendor near the landing stage.

'Who was that?' Joseph's son asked, his legs dangling from his chair.

'Nobody!' he was told. 'Stop asking questions, it's a bad habit.'

His mother pitched in:

'Eat!'

And everything sparkled, everything crackled, people and things, the light-coloured dresses, the plates, the dish of lamb, the lake and the sun, a blinding, chaotic universe, and in it the boy, clumsily holding his fork, searched for the extraordinary man who had just plunged into it.